A GRAVE RETURN

A DCI Luke Wiley Book

Jaye Bailey

PROLOGUE

She bursts out of the hotel room and walks as quickly as she can without breaking into a run towards the lift. She can't believe what has just happened.

Shaking her head, again and again, as a sort of confirmation of her own disbelief, she punches the elevator button. Punches it again.

She can not get out of there fast enough.

God, come on, she thinks. She has to get out of there.

The end of the conversation in the hotel room was unbearable. She had been lied to and above all, she had been very, very foolish. How could she have not seen this coming?

All of them were guilty. There was no avoiding it. But what had just happened in the hotel room made it difficult for her to breathe. Why was this happening to her? What was she going to do?

But she knows exactly what she was going to do – which was what she was going to do in the first place, before the text message that changed everything. What happened was no longer going to be a secret that they all carried to their graves. She would make sure of that.

———

The tears have finally come as she makes her way home. Disbelief has turned to anger, which has then turned slowly to sadness. She is exhausted and steps off the bus wearily, forcing herself to put one foot in front of the other for the last ten minutes of the journey between the bus stop and her front door. This has not been the evening she expected – all of the excitement she had felt as she left her flat had evaporated in an instant in that hotel room and into this mess of tears and the understanding that she will never have the life she wants. It isn't like her to find solace in revenge, but perhaps it is the only thing she has left now. Tomorrow. She will deal with everything tomorrow.

What she doesn't see is the person sitting on a bench on the green to the left of the pavement, about twenty feet in front of her. She doesn't understand that this person knows that she will cut across the green, even in the pitch dark, to save a few minutes of this journey home because she will be tired, and tearful and defeated. The green is deserted, the two figures are unseen, and it is the voice out of the dark that stops her cold. The voice is not a whisper – it is clear and calm.

'I've been waiting for you.'

The adrenaline that shoots through her body makes her breath catch and she wonders why she isn't already running. Why is she staring into the pitch black trying to see who is speaking to her? Where is the voice coming from?

The voice speaks again. 'You don't look okay.'

She steps closer, and finally sees who it is. Relief floods through her body when she realizes that she is not in danger, that she knows this voice.

'It's you. What are you doing here? You frightened me.'

'I need to speak to you. I think you are about to do something stupid.'

The tears begin to form again, this time from sheer frustration and she grimaces as she tries to force them back.

'Will you just stop it,' she says. 'I can't do this right now. This isn't up to you. You have no idea what I have just been through.'

She walks quickly away, not needing this – not needing any of what has happened tonight – towards the direction of her flat. She hears the reply, as clear and calm as before from behind her: 'This isn't up to you either. Why can't you leave it alone.'

The last sentence was not a question, it was a statement and she should have realized this. She should have been looking over her shoulder. She should have at least moved back onto the pavement because she does not see this figure move even more quickly than she is walking. Quickly up behind her and then suddenly she is dragged off her feet to the left in one violent, jerking movement. She cannot breathe.

She cannot breathe and she is being dragged further across the green towards the towering hedge that is about to obscure her from view. At first she thinks she is just winded but the air is not coming back into her lungs and she reaches for her throat. The band tightening around it is thin and slightly furry and she can't get her fingers beneath it. They slip over it and the band tightens more and more as she is dragged into the hedge. She desperately grabs at the ground, trying to stop her body from being hidden, then lashes out at the legs of the person holding the end of the ligature. She is truly gasping now, but there is no breath and no air and she is not making a sound as she begins to suffocate. She feels her face in the cool grass and the band around her throat tightens one more time as a shoe presses into her back with the last pull upwards and then everything goes dark.

ONE

Luke Wiley picked up his wristwatch from the kitchen counter where he had carefully laid it the evening before, and checked the second hand. His French press coffee maker sat on the counter in front of him, quietly – and perfectly – brewing his first cup of coffee of the day. The coffee maker was designed to maximize the oxygenation of the coffee grounds, which he had also whizzed up that morning from the slightly too expensive but delicious Guatemalan coffee beans purchased from Borough Market earlier in the week. The second hand moved around his wristwatch and when it reached the 12, Luke finally pressed down on the plunger. He poured a cup, added a dash of milk, brought it up to his face and inhaled.

Luke was precise, and he was particular and it used to drive his wife crazy.

'Why not grind the beans the night before? Save yourself the hassle in the morning – and most crucially, not wake me up?' she used to say.

But for Luke, precision was everything – and the taste of the coffee wouldn't be the same if he ground the beans the previous day. As for waking his wife, this no longer mattered as she was no longer there.

For most police detectives, coffee was a staple part of the diet and Luke was no exception to this. Caffeine got everyone through the day – it helped not only with concentration in a tricky job, but it also provided a dose of comfort when standing around a crime scene or when dealing with a victim became a bit too much. They were detectives, they were used to the often extremely grim nature of the job, but that didn't mean they weren't human. Luke liked to think of a cardboard cup of coffee pressed into his hand by a colleague as a sort of blanket – it was the cozy thing to hold onto when sometimes he felt lost on the job. The taste, however, was a completely different matter. That is why the first morning cup of coffee of the day was performed as a ritual – it might be the only decent cup of coffee he had for 24 hours.

But not these days.

Luke was coming close to the one year anniversary of leaving the Metropolitan Police Force. No longer was he Detective Inspector Wiley with his little office at headquarters just up from the Thames, no longer did he work with some of the best people he has ever known on some of the toughest homicide cases seen in the capital city, no longer did he live a life of right and wrong, good and bad. And the hardest thing of all – no longer did he come home at the end of a long day to his wife.

The first time Luke walked into this house, he audibly gasped. The house was an illusion – and how often now it felt like his wife was too. That Sadie existed as a sort of dream, a wonderful dream – but perhaps this was simply easier to believe instead of the reality that she was there and she was the best thing that had ever happened to him and now she was gone.

The house in Arlington Square looked like any other

house in the quadrangle of seemingly identical houses in the leafy part of Islington – all of the houses facing a beautiful little square with cherry blossom trees and four inward facing benches and dog walkers and newspaper readers and well dressed commuters making a short cut through the garden towards Upper Street and whatever bus was going to take them to the office.

He had been on two dates with Sadie and the third was dinner in the Draper's Arms. Ordinarily Luke didn't enjoy dating and had been perpetually single for years. Never someone to disappoint a friend, he had obliged many of them by agreeing to be set up, agreeing to the blind date and always happy to accompany someone at a wedding. He was the perfect plus one and seldom was there a weekend he wasn't invited out to dinner or to drinks by a raft of different friends. Sadie used to say that he could sit down at any table anywhere in the world and the hosts would be thrilled he was there – he could chat about any topic, he listened, he cared about everyone else's enjoyment around him. These were, of course, the best traits for a detective – equal parts awareness and empathy and an ease within himself that immediately made those around him feel comfortable too. These traits could also lead to errors, which Luke only knew too well.

Luke may have been always included in other peoples' social plans, but so was Sadie. And where Luke would walk into a room and move around it, making sure to meet everyone and chat with people in every corner, when Sadie entered a room she lit it up and would find herself rooted to the spot where she was handed her first glass. Because everyone in that room moved towards Sadie. It was like she had her own gravitational pull.

And on this third date, Luke was having the best time of his entire life. He couldn't get over that he was enjoying himself in this way, he couldn't stop laughing, he couldn't stop talking to this beautiful woman sitting across from him and wanted nothing more than to keep hearing her talk and then talk some more. So when the waiter shuffled over to them in the little corner at the back of the pub to ask if they would like the bill, they hadn't realized that they were the last people in the pub. All of the tables were cleared, their chairs over-turned and resting on top waiting for the floor to be swept. Sadie looked just as surprised as Luke was and suggested that they go back to hers for a nightcap.

'I'm right around the corner.'

'Oh. Great.'

As they stepped outside Sadie stopped and turned to him. Luke remembers the way she faced him and placed both palms flat against his chest, as if she was going to push him away. She smiled instead.

'This is the classic third date cliché. Inviting you back for a nightcap.'

'Oh, well, I mean, I don't...'

She stopped him by laughing. 'Don't worry. I can take care of myself.'

He didn't know it then, but this phrase would haunt him for the rest of his life.

Sadie walked up the little set of steps to her front door, unlocked it and went inside. As Luke followed her in, she hit the light switch and it wasn't the sudden brightness that stunned Luke, it was where he was standing and what he was looking at. This house wasn't the same as all of the other houses on the square, although it looked exactly the same from the outside. In fact, it wasn't one house at all. The external walls of the front of the house were a façade and hid the fact that this was two houses knocked through and Luke was standing in a vast internal courtyard. It wouldn't be until the morning that Luke understood he was actually at that moment standing underneath an enormous skylight that flooded the ground floor of the house with incredible light and that it felt as though you were standing outside. The property was stunning. It was unlike anything in London he had ever seen.

Sadie smiled at him. 'Come on in.'

Luke followed her through the house and into the kitchen with its granite counter tops and beautifully polished concrete floor. She turned to look at him and shrugged.

'We could do a bourbon or a green tea? Which is your preference?'

He didn't have one. He just wanted what she wanted. And he wanted her.

'I don't really mind. What are you in the mood for?'

'Oh I'm in the mood for both.'

He smiled at her and nodded and that is how she was – always in the mood for everything.

Luke stood now in that same kitchen, looking towards the garden although he couldn't see it because it was still dark outside. And he really, really missed his wife. He sipped his coffee and thought about his day and how on earth he was going to fill it.

There was a knock at the front door.

Luke looked at his watch, which was still lying on the kitchen counter. It was 5:45am.

There was only one person it could be.

Two

L uke opened the door to Detective Sargeant Hana Sawatsky, who was holding an empty coffee thermos, its lid in her other hand. She waved the thermos in front of Luke.

'No decent coffee in London at this time of the morning.'

Luke tried not to smile and stepped back to let Hana in.

'Also, you should be checking who is at the door before opening it,' Hana said, as she pushed past him and into the vast entrance.

Always a quip, always simultaneously looking after him – that was his ex-partner on the force.

'And good morning to you, too,' said Luke. They had been partners for five years before Luke unexpectedly left the service of the London Metropolitan Police almost a year ago. Instead of walking into the house towards the kitchen, something she had done a thousand times in a space where she felt right at home, she turned to Luke and put her hand on his arm.

'How are you doing? All okay?' Hana asked.

'I'm fine.'

'Okay,' she shrugged and shook her coffee cup again. 'I can smell the beans - you're bang on schedule.'

In the kitchen Hana poured herself a cup of coffee, opened the fridge and took out the milk. She poured the milk into her cup in an amount that would make you think: why the hell bother with the coffee? Luke said nothing but couldn't help shake his head. For years he had watched Hana do this, and on tough days he was happy to pour huge amounts of milk into her coffee himself, but he winced a bit thinking about the care he had just taken with those beans.

Hana stepped down into the large sunken dining part of the kitchen, which was completely enclosed by giant glass walls on every side. Sitting at her usual place at the kitchen table, she slid off her shoes and maneuvered to sit cross legged. Luke went to join her.

The size of the kitchen table made Hana appear smaller than she was, which was already pretty small. Luke remembered meeting her for the first time - she had been at a tough crime scene as a junior detective, still fresh to her role. A woman had been violently mugged and she was comforting the woman while the paramedics tended to her. The woman had, perhaps in shock, fought back a bit so her injuries were worse than they would have been had she let her phone and her bag simply be taken from her. Luke had been called to the scene and stepping out of his car, watched this small detective rub the back of the injured woman, telling her that she wasn't stupid for fighting back, that she would have done the same because it was instinct. Hana delicately reached up and brushed a tear from the woman's cheek with her own fingertip.

Out of seemingly nowhere, the second officer suddenly appeared, dragging the mugger in handcuffs towards them all. He wanted an ID from the woman, who confirmed that this was the man who had just attacked her. This was extremely lucky, and rare, to apprehend someone so quickly and so close to where the crime occurred,

The second officer nodded towards Luke, indicating that he was welcome to take over as the senior staff on the scene when Luke suddenly felt a hand on his chest, as if to hold him back. Puzzled, he turned to see Hana Sawatsky — a detective he outranked, and someone he had never met — her hand on his chest, suddenly push past him towards the mugger. She stood in front of him and then with the strength of a man three times her size, pick him up by the elbow, twisting him backwards and slamming him into the side of the patrol car to search him herself. Luke watched Hana lean up and forward and whisper something into the mugger's ear, before calmly turning and saying to Luke, 'Thank you, sir. All yours.' She ran her hand through her brunette bob, returned to the woman, stepped into the ambulance with her and watched Luke through the rear ambulance window as it pulled away.

Luke was impressed, and surprised, and pursed his lips together in the way that he always did when he was secretly pleased about something — a gesture he was completely unaware of. It had been a masterclass in tough, empathetic policing - something all too rare in the force these days and when Luke suddenly was in need of a detective at a case one month later, he looked back through the case notes to figure out what her name was and Hana Sawatsky entered his life on a basis that he didn't know at the time would be quite so permanent. There was a lot he still had to learn about Hana Sawatsky.

'I miss her, you know. I mean, I miss her all the time, but especially when I'm here in the house sitting with you,' said Hana.

'I know. Me too.'

'I still get this weird thing when I walk up the steps to the door — it happened just now. For a split second I thought she was going to open it.'

Luke nodded and looked down at his coffee.

'Yeah, I know.'

'So,' Luke said. 'Are you starting or finishing your shift? Or just wanted to turn up here at 5:45 in the morning?'

'Just needed a coffee, mate.'

'Right.'

There was a pause.

'I'm working now, actually. A woman has been found murdered in Parsons Green. Lots of chatter about it on the radio.'

'You know I don't work for the Met anymore?'

'I just thought I should let you know.'

'Hana, what the hell? It's a little early, even for you.' Hana shuffled in her chair.

'It's just that someone is about to ring your doorbell,' she said.

'What? Why?'

There was another long pause and Hana looked at him. 'They are coming to pick you up and bring you in.'

Luke laughed. 'What on earth are you talking about?'

'I don't know. I just heard that Luke Wiley was to be picked up and brought in.'

'I don't get it, Hana. I don't work there anymore. And why would they want me brought in?'

Hana took a sip of her coffee. 'Something's not right. I don't know.'

'Something's not right? Are you kidding me? And you've been here having a chat for ten minutes before saying anything?'

Hana smiled and began to put her shoes back on.

'Well Luke, what did you always say?'
Luke shook his head and muttered to himself.
'Never lead with the best part.'

THREE

Michael McPherson isn't exactly frantic, but he is beginning to feel extremely flustered. He can't find his phone. He woke with a headache and after gulping down the glass of water siting on his bedside table, he reached for it as usual. But there was the wireless charging mat, sitting empty.

His head felt a bit fuzzy and he took a moment to piece together where he had been last night. Who he had been with. This is when he began to feel flustered.

Michael turned to face the other side of the bed and it was empty. His wife was already up, although he heard only silence downstairs. She must have gone out, early morning Saturday grocery shopping probably. The silence emanating from the bedrooms of his two sons was no surprise. At thirteen and fifteen years old, they would not be emerging for some time.

Throwing on a robe and shoving his feet into a worn pair of slippers, he padded quietly downstairs, poking his head into the tv room on his way. His phone wasn't there either.

He was surprised not to see any coffee made already. Lottie usually wouldn't do anything without making herself a flat white first - the ridiculous milk foamer that Michael hated the sound of, usually lying in the sink unwashed for much of the day.

He moved towards the front of the house and looked out at the street. The car was missing, so she had driven somewhere. It also meant that he'd hear her parking and car doors slamming before she entered the house, so he had time unobserved to look for his phone.

A quick scan of the kitchen brought up nothing. He cursed that they had cancelled the house's landline earlier that year, ostensibly because no one really used it anymore, but really because it was a cost-cutting measure. He couldn't call his phone to hear it ring from its hiding place, and he didn't want to wake either of his sons up by creeping into their rooms and using theirs, surely lost somewhere in their bedsheets or tossed under a bed before crashing out.

He sighed heavily. How he would have loved to open his iPad and press the app for 'Find My Phone'. But, of course, this function had been wiped from his phone several months earlier out of necessity.

As Michael filled the espresso machine with water, he thought back to the previous evening. Friday night. He had, for once, been invited out for drinks with the guys from the trading floor. He tried not to show his delight with being asked to tag along, to be included with these guys. He had always planned to be a trader, but hadn't done well as a trainee at the financial firm when he finished university. He knew that his bosses didn't feel he had what it took to succeed in that cut-throat world. He wasn't ever going to be the money maker. Instead, he was shunted into the research side of the firm and he was still there fifteen years later. But Michael was still as crucial to their fragile, money making ecosystem - without his reports about the state of the commodities the traders were buying and selling, no one would be making any money at all. He was excellent at running these reports — for which he could have received a little more thanks. Michael tried to think if he had texted Lottie to say he was going out and would be late home. Did he have his phone then?

The traders made a lot more money than he did - their salaries and bonuses eye-watering compared to his, so the after-work venue was all about double digit cocktails and triple digit bottles of champagne. Michael hadn't lasted too long and after two drinks he reluctantly made his excuses and left.

They had barely spoken to him anyway. How arrogant they were, with their bespoke suits and designer watches that they had to be on waitlists to purchase. He wondered why they had invited him in the first place? He felt wounded thinking that he had perhaps just been in the way when plans were being set up for the evening. He had overheard and they were simply being polite by asking him.

Michael knew that his time would come — he quietly traded his own stocks from the office he set up for himself in the back garden shed. They would have laughed at him if they'd known - and he had been unlucky as of late, losing more money than he could ever dare telling Lottie about, but he was close to turning his luck around. He knew he would privately beat them at their own game.

This didn't stop him from feeling pissed off at the whole situation — their lack of acknowledgement of what he did and his temporary lack of funds — so he didn't head straight home. He couldn't bear it. Everything in his life felt like a mess and the last person he wanted to see was his wife. A couple of blocks away was a pub, more at his price point, and he went in to sit at the bar and have a pint. He couldn't remember how long he had stayed there.

His coffee poured, Michael was about to head out into the garden and see how his stocks were performing overnight when he heard a car door slam. He turned around and opened the front door for Lottie, who wasn't carrying grocery bags as he expected, but was dressed in yoga pants and a sweatshirt, her coat thrown over the top, and she looked like she had been rushing around.

'Where have you been?' Michael asked.

'Drycleaning. Had to drop something off.'

'Early on a Saturday morning?'

'Yes, Michael.' Lottie sighed and pushed past him into the house. 'There's something I need to wear next week that wasn't clean.'

'Right. Well, did you pick up my shirts then?'

'What?'

'My shirts?' Michael raised his eyebrows. 'Did you collect them?'

'No, I'll do it next week.'

Lottie tucked her hair behind her ears and quickly took off her coat, throwing it over the kitchen counter. She sighed and looked at her husband.

'What, Michael. I have things to do here.'

Michael looked at her, feeling nothing but irritation. She hadn't asked anything about his evening or how he was that morning. As usual, he was some sort of appendage in his wife's life, a life that neither of them seemingly wanted to be in together.

'Have you seen my phone?'

Lottie shook her head and she took a coffee mug out of the cupboard and began to fiddle with the espresso machine.

'Are you sure?'

Lottie stopped what she was doing, looked at her husband and sighed again.

———

At the end of the McPherson's backyard, in the garden shed that makes up Michael's little home office — with his computer and oversized monitor, his files, a meticulously curated stationery set — is his desk. And on his desk is his phone, its screen illuminated with over a dozen missed calls. The phone is on silent.

On the other side of London, Lucy Bishop is dialling Michael's number. She guesses that his phone is on silent but is desperately praying that he will see the notifications or turn it back on. The phone keeps ringing before it goes to voice-mail, so it isn't switched off. Why the hell isn't he answering? With this many missed calls, and after everything that is at risk with them all, he would not be ignoring her on purpose. There is too much at stake.

Finally, she rings the one other person she knows will maybe be able to help. He has everything to lose, too.

When he answers on the first ring, Lucy is flooded with relief.

'Oh thank god you answered.'

'Lucy.' The man's voice cut her off.

'Yes?'

He didn't even need to explain except to say, 'I've been calling him all night. Something is wrong.'

FOUR

New Scotland Yard loomed in front of Luke and he found himself counting his breaths, in and out, as he walked towards the entrance. It had been just over a year since he last walked through these doors.

He wasn't nervous or anxious about stepping back inside police headquarters, if anything he felt curious about why he was here, but there was something about the sight of the fading white concrete, the opaque windows glinting in the sun and the hum of the traffic on the Embankment behind him that began to bring everything back.

The officers who had turned up at Luke's house weren't exactly forthcoming. They wouldn't give a reason that Luke was to be brought into the station. But it was also clear that this wasn't a request. Hana offered to take Luke to the station in her car, and also made it clear that this was not a request. She outranked the officers who shuffled awkwardly on Luke's front steps and they quickly agreed.

Hana and Luke were mostly silent in the car on the fifteen minute journey from leafy north London down towards the river. They so often sat in silence like this now, both of them probably as aware as the other of how different everything felt.

'You ready?' said Hana as she moved towards the revolving glass doors, looking towards Luke. He found himself reaching into his back pocket for his key card to let himself through the security barrier, but of course he no longer had a key card. Force of habit was one thing, Luke's renowned, obsessive force of habit — often laughed about on the force — was another.

Hana dealt with the guest protocol at reception and they walked into the central elevator together.

'Is it weird?' she asked as the elevator ferried them up to one of the top floors.

'So weird.'

'Yeah. Sorry.'

The elevator doors opened on floor seven and the familiar sight of the reception desk leading to Serious Crime Command and Met Intelligence was in front of him. And leaning on the desk was Laura Rowdy — purveyor of intelligence, compiler of data, sorter of evidence — whatever you needed found to crack a case, Laura Rowdy was the person to do it. In Luke's opinion, the Metropolitan Police Force would not function without her.

'Hey, Rowdy.'

Laura looked up and stared at him.

'Oh my god. Luke.'

She rushed towards him and grasped his hands, each with one of her own.

'What on earth are you doing here?' Rowdy said. And then she shook her head as if to indicate it was crazy that those words had even came out of her mouth. The past year had been so hard for all of them — what had happened in the case that broke Luke Wiley couldn't help but break the rest of them, too. Luke should be standing there. He used to walk off that elevator every day and greet her with a wink and a smile

and very often a squeeze of the shoulder. He was always warm
with the colleagues he liked, the ones he respected, and it was
hard — even for tough as nails Laura Rowdy — to not be just
a little bit in love with Luke Wiley.

'You tell me, Rowdy. I've been picked up and brought in.'

'Is this true?' Rowdy asked, looking towards Hana.

Hana nodded her head.

'No idea either, Rowdy.'

By this time, the familiar patter of Luke, Hana and
Rowdy's voices were echoing down the hall and the heads of
those already in the office at this early hour were poking out to
see if, in fact, what they were hearing was actually real. Luke
greeted a couple of his old colleagues, feeling more and more
uneasy as the seconds passed. Something didn't feel right.

'Do you know who I'm actually supposed to be seeing,
Hana?'

'Let me check.'

Luke and Rowdy chatted to each other at the reception
desk as Hana went off to inquire as to where and why any of
this was happening at all. She swallowed hard as she walked
back towards Luke.

'It's O'Donnell. You're here to see O'Donnell.'

'You've got to be kidding me,' said Luke.

Luke, Hana and Rowdy looked at each other, none of
them speaking.

'Jesus Christ,' Luke muttered under his breath. 'Well, let's
get this over with.'

Chief Inspector Stephen O'Donnell had been Luke's boss
for the past several years. He was everyone's boss on this floor
of Scotland Yard. He could probably be best described by
everything he was not. He wasn't remarkable, he didn't stand
out in a room, he wasn't interesting, he inspired absolutely no
one. He had a habit of puffing his chest out and leaning
forward when trying to make a point and was known for

raising his voice with an Irish lilt when irritated. This was quite something to behold as contrary to his last name, Stephen O'Donnell had likely never step foot in Ireland in his life.

When Luke was promoted and transferred to Serious Crime, his new boss had been described to him by a colleague as someone who spectacularly failed upwards. Luke hadn't been particularly bothered by this description — he'd encountered his fair share of these kinds of people in his line of work. But he quickly discovered that this wasn't exactly the case. O'Donnell could be clever and when he saw others doing well, this could slide quickly into cruelty. Stephen O'Donnell's problem wasn't that he was lazy or dim, his problem was that he was a prick.

'I'm coming with you,' Hana said as she and Luke and Rowdy walked down the corridor towards the hub of the unit.

'Not a good idea,' said Luke. 'Let me handle this and then let's go get another coffee. Where the hell is he?'

And then Stephen O'Donnell puffed his way out of his office, extending a hand towards Luke. Surprised, Luke shook it and nodded at his old boss.

'Thanks for coming in, Luke. I'm sorry that the officers had to bother you so early in the morning.'

'It's okay. I was up.'

'After you,' O'Donnell said, pointing towards the meeting room that sat towards the rear of the floor. The room was typically used only for serious meetings and uncomfortable conversations. It was enclosed by windows on one side that overlooked the maze of little streets behind Scotland Yard and the front glass faced the unit. It was intelligent glass, able to be switched from crystal clear to opaque at the touch of a button.

Would O'Donnell dare to touch that button, Luke wondered. He sat down in a chair facing towards the unit. He looked towards Hana and Rowdy who were staring back at him, probably wondering the same thing.

Luke looked at O'Donnell, silently daring him to do it. O'Donnell walked towards the wall and pressed the button before moving towards the chair opposite Luke and sitting down. Luke couldn't help but chuckle aloud.

'Yes?' O' Donnell said.

They stared at each other.

'Why the hell am I here, Stephen.'

'How have you been Luke?'

'I've been just fine. Can we get on with it?'

'It's been, what, a year since you so abruptly left us?'

'Thirteen months.'

'Ah, already thirteen months is it? Thirteen months of having to pick up everything you just dropped when you went.'

'Is this what this is about, Stephen?' Luke leaned back in his chair. 'You want to have a go at me for leaving? I think you know the situation. I think everything was extremely clear.'

'Oh it was clear alright, Wiley. Crystal god damn clear and the inquiry surrounding your mess is still ongoing.'

What was Luke supposed to say to that? He had no good answer to give. So he swallowed and tried one more time.

'What am I doing here?'

'Where were you last night, Wiley?'

'At home.'

'Alone at home?'

Luke visibly bristled. His chest tightened as it often did now, as if he could get very little air when he tried to breathe.

'Yes. I was alone at home.'

'Are you sure? No one new since Sadie?'

All of the air in Luke's body seemed to rush out of him at once. It was as if O'Donnell's words had physically winded him and he gripped the edge of the table.

Luke spoke very slowly. 'Crystal god damn clear.'

O'Donnell seemed to grimace and puffed out his chest.

'How do you know Chloe Little?'

'Who?'

'Chloe Little.'

Luke took a moment to think. Usually he had excellent recall for names and faces, but recently who knows what his brain was capable of remembering. He wanted to close his eyes for a second, something to help him fly through the rolodex in his head. An old case? A friend of Sadie's he had forgotten about? He couldn't think quickly enough.

'Nothing to say, Wiley?'

Luke looked at him. 'I don't believe I know a Chloe Little. Why are you asking?'

'Because she was found murdered in Parsons Green yesterday evening.'

Luke couldn't help but laugh. 'I'm sorry, Stephen. Yes, you are absolutely right. I have given up my career as a Detective Chief Inspector and taken up a new one. Murderer.'

'Do you really think this is the time to be funny?'

'Jesus Christ, Stephen. Will you just get on with it.'

It was at this point that O'Donnell began to smile, and Luke knew that smile all too well. It was a smile that made the corners of O'Donnell's mouth pinch downwards as his eyes glinted.

From the file next to him, O'Donnell pulled out a piece of paper with a woman's face on it. It was clearly taken from a driver's license - something that Laura Rowdy had probably pulled up from the database and printed out. The woman looked to be in her thirties, brunette, quite striking, even in a driver's license photograph.

'Chloe Little?' Luke asked.

O'Donnell said nothing and pulled something else out of the file. It was another piece of paper with a photograph printed on it. Except this one was in an evidence bag. He tossed it on the table in front of Luke.

Luke's mouth involuntarily opened, but no sound came out. He couldn't believe what he was looking at. It was a slightly grainy photograph, but very clearly a photograph of Luke Wiley.

'Where did you get this?'

'From Chloe Little,' O'Donnell smirked. 'She was carrying it when she was murdered.'

FIVE

Luke and Hana walked out of New Scotland Yard by the back entrance. Her car was parked around the corner in its usual spot and they didn't walk towards it, but rather to the cafe just opposite to pick up another coffee as they always used to do.

The cafe owner raised his eyebrows when he saw Luke walk in the door, then turned to begin making his cortado without even asking.

'So what the hell, Luke. What happened in there?'

'I need to get in Chloe Little's home. Do you know where it is?'

'Is that the name of the victim? Chloe Little? I brought you straight to the station. I haven't spoken to anyone. I don't have the details.'

'Yes. And she clearly knew who I am.'

'Why do you think this?'

'O'Donnell threw an evidence bag down in front of me. It had my photo in it, taken from the victim's possessions.'

'From her house?'

'No. It was on her. That's why I need to get into that house.'

Hana took her milky coffee, forced a lid on top and was on her phone before they had even stepped outside again.

With the address in hand, they began to make their way through morning rush hour traffic in central London. It was slow, but it gave them time to consider what has happening.

'Her name doesn't ring a bell with you?'

'No,' said Luke. 'And Rowdy had clearly pulled up her driver license photo — I have never seen her before.'

'Are you sure?'

Luke looked over at Hana.

'Pretty sure, but I can't help but...' He trailed off.

Hana knew what the end of that sentence contained. Luke wanted to say, 'I can't help but doubt myself.' But she left it alone - it was too painful for him, and doubt was the last thing either of them needed right now. They needed clear heads and confidence in order to best look at everything in front of them.

'Are you sure you don't want to go to the medical examiner first?' asked Hana. 'They are bound to have some answers by now.'

'No. Definitely need the house. There was something about the photo.'

'What? Something apart from the fact that it was a photo of you?'

'Yes. It was printed on a sheet of paper, like it had been taken from something off the internet. I don't know. We can search for what it came from later. But for now I need to get in that house. The paper had a pinhole in the top of it. Like she had it pinned up somewhere.'

Hana slowly exhaled. Luke's eye for detail clearly wasn't in doubt. He still had it.

————

The leafy green spaces of west London became more frequent as they got closer to Parsons Green. The Green itself was still cordoned off as officers combed the expanse inch by inch looking for evidence of the horrific murder that had taken place only hours previously. But they turned left, towards the Thames and down a quiet street of beautiful terraced houses. Only the expensive members only tennis club sat between these equally expensive houses and the river.

'It's like your neighbourhood,' said Hana. It wasn't a judgement or a snide remark, but the first comment of observation.

They pulled up on the road and parked. Hana strode towards the cordon and flashed her badge at the officer standing guard.

'He's with me,' Hana thrust her thumb towards Luke and Luke went to lift the ribbon to duck underneath.

'I'm sorry, Sir. Police only at this point.'

Luke looked at him and closed his eyes, waiting for Hana to explode. But before she could open her mouth, they heard a low, booming voice shout towards their direction.

'Let them through, officer.'

Oh thank god, Luke thought. A friendly face, that of Detective Inspector Hackett.

'Hackett. Good to see you.'

'You, too, Wiley.'

Hackett strode towards them, all six feet six inches of him. Never a particular smiley man, he was nevertheless unfailingly pleasant, hardworking and amiable. He had risen the police ranks with Luke, always there but never competitive. They had always got along well and Luke felt a rush of relief seeing him standing there.

'Shall we?' Hackett said, gesturing towards the front door of Chloe Little's house, moving Luke and Hana away from the heavier police presence at the cordon tape so they could speak without being overheard.

'I want to say that I'm surprised to see you here, Wiley, but of course I'm not.'

Luke nodded.

'What's the story so far, Hackett?'

'Well, I wasn't actually assigned here. I heard on the radio that you were to be picked up and brought in. Couldn't help but get to the scene and see what the hell was going on. As I'm sure you know, it's just up the road and now I've taken over the initial search of the victim's house. Get suited up and then come in. We haven't found much yet.'

Hackett called over a member of the forensics team, who handed Luke and Hana protective shoe coverings and latex gloves, which they slipped on before stepping inside the front door.

Hackett closed the door behind him and the quiet and stillness of the house immediately enveloped them. It was peaceful inside and felt calm. Luke studied the front hall of the house as Hackett began to run them through what he knew.

'Chloe Little was 36 years old. Lawyer. Lived here alone and was either on her way home or on her way out somewhere before she was killed. Where she was found is the short cut between here and the tube station.'

'When was she found?'

'1:25am. A young man was cutting through the green on his way home from a night out and spotted her. He called 999.'

'Was she lying on on the green in plain view?' asked Hana.

'No. She had been dragged into the bushes to the east side of the green. We questioned the guy and he said he had the flashlight on his phone on and it picked up part of her in the bushes. He was pretty shaken up to have discovered her. We took him to the station for prints and ID check, but he wouldn't be my first port of call.'

'How was she killed?'

'Not clear,' Hackett said. 'But I'd guess strangled. She's been with the coroner now for a couple of hours, so we'll have more information later today.'

Luke looked at them both, with raised eyebrows.

'No ligature left with the body?'

'Not on the body and nothing recovered at the scene.'

'So not a crime of chance,' Luke said. 'What else did you find with the victim?'

'Not a lot, I'm afraid. No bag or phone. Her house keys were in her trouser pocket and I assume you've seen what was in her coat pocket?'

Luke nodded. 'Yes, O'Donnell had the pleasure of showing me.'

Hackett looked at Luke and Hana, hoping for some sort of explanation.

'Your guess is as good as ours, Sir, ' said Hana.

'Right. Well, take a look around. We're dusting and we've taken her laptop which was in the office at the back of the house, just past the kitchen. Honestly, I'm not sure what we are looking for yet. But check in before you go.'

'Thanks, Hackett.'

Hackett nodded and let himself out the front door as Luke and Hana began to make their way through the ground floor of the house.

'How is he so sure that Chloe Little lived here alone?' murmured Luke, as he began to do what he always did when walking through a new space for the first time, looking for answers hidden among the pieces of furniture, the knick-knacks on shelves and bureaus, the spaces in a life unknown to him for now. He quietly talked to himself. They settled back into their own, familiar roles like the past thirteen months had never happened. Hana walked beside him, slightly more slowly, breathing in the house as if she was the one living there. What was out of place if this was her living room? What didn't seem right?

'Everything is extremely ordered and neat here, Luke. She definitely lived here alone. Men aren't this tidy.'

'My house looks like this.'

'Yes, and you aren't normal.'

Luke looked over at her and rolled his eyes.

It was an average sized terraced house and while many on this street would have had walls knocked down to create larger open plan spaces that incorporated a kitchen and dining room, Chloe's house still had the slightly smaller individual rooms. The living room was beautifully decorated — the walls a light maple colour, framed paintings under brass antique picture lights on each wall. The sofa was a beautiful soft blue velvet, a grey leather chair to its right and between them a large glass coffee table. The coffee table was covered in expensive photography books, art gallery catalogues, a Diptyque candle that had never been lit. Everything was aligned and perfect, like it was about to be shot for a magazine spread.

'This room doesn't look lived in,' said Hana. 'It's like she's waiting to impress someone with it.'

'Lots of photos though,' Luke pointed towards the fireplace. There were half a dozen framed photographs on the mantel — all in identical thin silver frames. Luke adjusted his gloves and began to pick them up one by one to study. The photographs all featured Chloe — she was strikingly beautiful, standing out amongst the other girls that flanked her in each photo.

'Is there a sibling in these?' asked Luke, probably unaware that he had said the words aloud.

'Maybe one of these girls is a sister. But these are definitely girls trips.'

Chloe Little was a little younger in a couple of the photographs — they must have spanned a decade or so, but in every photograph she is beaming — with friends in front of Sagrada Familia in Barcelona, sipping straws sticking out of coconuts on a white sandy beach, hanging out of a green jeep with an elephant behind her.

'These are expensive holidays, Luke.'

'No kidding. Fits the house and job though.'

They walked into the next room, the dining room, which looked pristine.

'No one ate in here last night,' said Hana as she opened the sideboard to look inside. Serving dishes, wine glasses of varying sizes and flatware filled the unit, probably enough to comfortably serve ten people around the large table.

The kitchen was just as clean and organized, the counters home to what looked like a well-used Kitchenaid mixer, ceramic jars filled with lentils and oats and sugar and a glass filled with whisks and spatulas.

'Well, she definitely cooks.'

Luke was staring inside the cupboard to the right of the refrigerator and it was stacked with dozens of spice jars.

'You'd think these would be in perfect glass jars with identical labels for show like the rest of the house. But she is using these,' he said.

Luke opened each of the cupboard doors and checked behind the main kitchen door into the hallway.

'No cork board?' said Hana.

He shook his head and they continued on to try to find what they were looking for, even if they didn't know what it was yet.

'Here,' Luke said as they finally entered a room that looked more like someone actually lived in this house. The final room on the ground floor was set up as a home office and tv room. A comfy looking, slightly worn sofa sat in the middle of the room as a kind of divider, facing bookshelves and the flat screen television that was mounted on the wall above them. The rest of the room was taken up with a large wooden desk, filing cabinet and printer. They guessed that the laptop had been taken from this desk, as the USB cable that connected to the printer was left sitting on top of the filing cabinet. Hana tried the cabinet but it was locked.

'I'll ask Hackett if they've tried to get into this yet,' she said and left Luke staring at what he had been hoping to find.

A small, cheap cork board was fixed to a part of the wall that jutted out next to the desk. Round silver pins sat pushed into the board, all lined up in an even row. The only item attached to the board was a faded receipt and warranty guarantee for the printer.

Luke shook his head. 'Damnit,' he said softly.

'What were you hoping was there?' Hana said, having returned to the office.

'I don't know. But something. Do they have a key to the filing cabinet?'

'Not yet.'

'Damn. Okay. Let's look upstairs?'

The top floor of the house contained two bedrooms, a large bathroom and a smaller one that had been converted into a laundry room. To the left of the staircase was the guest bedroom and like the rooms downstairs was immaculate.

'God, I'd have this bathroom,' said Hana as she looked around it. It was completely tiled in white and had both a claw foot bathtub and a walk-in rain shower. A giant fern in a terracotta pot stood in the corner and it was resplendent, obviously delighted to live in a steamy room and directly underneath a large skylight.

Hana bent down and touched the floor with her gloved palm.

'I knew it. Heated floor. God, this is nice.'

And like the other rooms, it was tidy. All of Chloe's toiletries and sundries that in Hana's flat would have been scattered around the bathroom were neatly put in their place in the large mirrored cabinet.

The final room to check was Chloe's bedroom and when Luke and Hana walked into it, they were both silent as they took everything in.

The bed was made, but clothes were strewn everywhere. A dress was draped over the back of a chair, two pairs of trousers and various coloured tights had been thrown on the bed. The closet door was open, revealing a full length mirror behind it and Luke had to step over different shoes scattered across the floor, clearly tried on and kicked off many times over.

'Well, she was clearly going somewhere in a hurry,' said Hana.

Luke surveyed the room very slowly with his eyes, taking everything in.

He shrugged. 'Or she was just indecisive.'

'The woman with a house that looks like this was indecisive? I don't think so, Luke.'

He nodded. 'Exactly.'

Chloe Little had been heading off somewhere either with little notice, or with a lot of anticipation. Or she had already been there and was on her way back. Luke walked over to the window and looked outside. It was always the most ordinary scenes that housed the deepest secrets. Chloe Little certainly had one, and one that involved him. He didn't like it and as he looked at Hana, equally perplexed, he knew that she didn't like it either.

'Let's see what else Hackett has to say.'

Luke and Hana left Chloe's bedroom to the forensic team

and headed back downstairs. Had they looked a little bit longer out of the bedroom window, they might have seen a woman around Chloe's age across the street and a couple of houses away staring at Chloe's house in disbelief. They would have seen her fingering the set of house keys in her hand and then quickly turning to walk back towards the river making sure that she hadn't been seen.

Six

The whole night had been awful. After the phone call, Lucy couldn't sleep at all and eventually stopped even trying. Her argument on the phone with Chloe had been the final straw in an incredibly distressing day. How dare Chloe think she could make decisions on behalf of all of them? It was outrageous and just completely like Chloe. Always thinking she knew best, always having to take over a conversation, always needing to be the one in control. Lucy had absolutely had enough. They were supposed to be friends and this is not how friends should be treated.

Her flat was cold and Lucy was freezing so she dragged her duvet with her from the bedroom to the sitting room, creating a little nest on her small sofa to crawl into. She wanted to make a hot cup of tea but the thought of leaving the duvet to stand in the cold kitchen waiting for the kettle to boil was too much. Everything felt like it was too much at the moment.

She flicked through the tv channels for a bit, hoping to find something to distract her but there was nothing decent to watch. She sighed and picked up her phone. There were three voicemails that she had been ignoring, having looked at her phone each time it rang and watching the phone until the ringing stopped and eventually the voicemail icon popped up on the screen.

She had an idea of what the messages said but she listened to them anyway. They were all from her younger brother and the first two messages were to see where she was — she was late for her nephew's tenth birthday party. Was she okay? Was she going to make it? Lucy had, in fact, been sitting right where she sat now, nowhere near her brother's lovely house, being welcomed in by his tedious but polite wife, surrounded by a gaggle of bouncing, yelling ten year olds. Her nephew was sweet and a rather interesting little boy, so she felt a bit guilty about not being there. But she had sent a card and that was the best she could do.

It was the third voicemail that would be the interesting one. She put this one on speaker so her brother's voice filled her dark, cold sitting room.

'Lucy. Look - I know that you feel things are unfair and I know you are pissed off. But what I think is unfair is that you are taking it out on us. Do you not want to be a part of your own family? Family is important. I think you need to re-evaluate that. Call me back.'

What an asshole, Lucy thought. He had no idea what it was like for her, and worse, had no clue that his role in their whole sorry family saga was a factor in what had happened.

She had been close to her brother when they were growing up, or at least they got along. Lucy was five years older and when Lucy was fifteen and her brother was ten, just the age her nephew was now, their father died. It was sudden and unexpected and overnight their mother had to cope with a life that overwhelmed her. Lucy seemed to become the focus of everything that had gone wrong in her mother's life — as a teenager she couldn't do anything right and somehow her brother was perfect in her mother's eyes. Decades later, nothing had really changed.

It had been incredibly painful — for Lucy it felt as if her mother didn't really want to know her, but instead invested all of her emotional energy in her brother. She supposed that this wasn't unique to their family — didn't every parent have a favourite even if they wouldn't admit it? But then the finances began to be lopsided as well. What began as a kind of small ache within her from being ignored bloomed into a deep, unrelenting anger. As Lucy graduated from the local school, funds were suddenly made available for her brother to attend the astronomically expensive boarding school two counties over. Of course he excelled there - having been given every opportunity to do so. But Lucy persevered. She put herself through university working long hours after classes. She got funding to do a masters degree in education and her career was fulfilling. After years of teaching in underprivileged schools, working with children to unleash their potential in often very difficult circumstances, she had been appointed as the head of an excellent elementary school with a great reputation. It had been a struggle, but Lucy always felt that it had been worth it. There was a part of her that wanted to prove to her mother that she was just as worthy as her brother.

She shouldn't have had the thought as it made her uncomfortable — but how could she help it — that finally when her mother died she would at least inherit half of her estate. It wouldn't be an enormous amount of money, but it would finally give her enough to buy a flat and she could say goodbye to the endless cycle of damp rentals and dodgy landlords. And Lucy felt that it may just make up for everything she had lost in the difficult relationship she endured with her mother.

A little over a year ago, her mother did die. She shouldn't have been surprised at what happened, but she was. Her brother got absolutely everything.

'But it's not what I had planned either,' he said to her. 'This isn't my fault.'

And it wasn't even that blatant. It wasn't the kind of will that would have people gasping at the unfairness of it all. Money had been left for her nephew's education and with private school fees being what they are and the possibility of an expensive university education as well, that's where all the money went. Lucy had spoken to her brother with what she thought was a fair and gentle approach. Things had been unequal for quite some time and with his salary he could maybe pay the tuition fees for his son himself? Perhaps Lucy could be given some of this money? Didn't that seem fair?

Lucy can picture him now as she sits in the dark, the tv screen flickering on mute in front of her.

'Luce, this isn't really up to me. It's what mum wanted. I'm sorry. I can't help you.'

————

I'm sorry. I can't help you. She couldn't get his voice out of her head. She had called Chloe and sobbed down the phone. Their lives were different in so many ways, but she always felt that Chloe understood her. If they understood each other, how could Chloe be so heartless now? Their argument had been terrible — she had wanted to talk about her brother, not have Chloe take over everything. Lucy tried to put it out of her mind.

When she woke hours later in her duvet nest on the sitting room sofa, she felt uneasy. The content of the conversation with Chloe the previous night had been unsettling. She decided she had best ring Michael to get his opinion, but then he wasn't answering his phone. In desperation she called Nigel, who was honestly the last person she wanted to speak to first thing in the morning, but she didn't know what else to do. When Nigel said that he had been calling Michael all night but that he hadn't answered, Lucy's unease began to escalate. She couldn't just sit there in her flat, so she threw on some clothes and began to make her way over to Chloe's. She guessed that Michael might already be there and he would know what to do. Either way, they all needed to get together and figure out what they were going to do.

It wasn't far from Earls Court to Chloe's road just off Parsons Green. A couple of stops on the District Line and then a ten minute walk down towards the river. There was a slight bend in Chloe's road, which is why she didn't see the police cordon until she was almost at the house. She stopped cold. Were they at Chloe's? She felt her breath catch as she realized that was exactly where the police were coming in and out of. A small crowd of onlookers had gathered next to her, walking from the opposite direction. Lucy turned quickly and began striding back towards where she had just come from.

Oh god, she thought.

Her hands shaking she tried calling Michael one more time, already knowing that he was not going to answer.

Seven

Hana makes a call as soon as they are back in her car. Laura Rowdy confirms that she has both the CCTV from the tube station and Chloe Little's registered mobile phone number, even though they are still missing her phone. The records were being pulled up as they were speaking.

'Do you want to come back to the station with me?'

'Best not. I don't think O'Donnell is going to want to see me in there again today, uninvited.'

Luke looks at his watch. 'I'm seeing Nicky later this morning anyway.'

'Do you want me to drop you off?'

Luke looked at his watch again. 'I'm a little early, but thanks. You can drop me at Victoria Station on your way back. I'll hop on the tube up to Highbury.'

'Sure,' Hana smiled. All the money Luke had and he was going to take the tube home. If Hana had Luke's wealth, she would be in a warm, comfortable taxi but there you go. He was a peculiar creature, Hana thought to herself as they sped along the Embankment towards Victoria. Buy only bespoke, tailored jackets — sure. Take a taxi for twenty quid home on a cold day — no way. It was good to be with Luke today as they used to be. She had missed him.

As they pulled up to Victoria Station and Luke opened the car door, Hana confirmed that she would get the latest update and then give him a call.

'Thanks, Hana.'

The tube sped north, deep below the web of buildings and loud traffic and frenetic energy of central London. Luke stood in the centre of a packed carriage, holding onto the dangling handle above him, letting his body sway in time with the movement of the train. He was lost in himself, thinking about the bewildering morning and simultaneously thrilled to be looking at a case again. He wished he did not feel this way.

As passengers jostled each other getting on and off the train, irritated with the morning rush hour, Luke was oblivious to everyone around him. The Victoria Line was always cramped and uncomfortable, but it was fast and Luke was startled to hear the announcement for Highbury Station. He politely pushed his way off the train and ascended up to street level. The day was crisp and cool but sunny and Luke loved these kinds of days. His mind was whirring with the open ended possibilities of a case, the weather was ideal for walking and thinking and it was still the morning, so lots of time ahead of him for the day to unfold. It would have been the perfect kind of day except for the one unavoidable thing that was missing.

The panic that began to slowly rise from the top of his ribcage into the bottom of his throat announced itself as it always did when he began to think about it. He quickened his pace and weaved his way through the winding streets of High-bury towards Nicky's house.

Dr. Nicky Bowman lived in a house that would have more closely resembled Luke's, had Luke's house not actually been two houses knocked into one giant property. She lived one neighbourhood up and to the east of Luke's, which looking back is probably the only thing that made visiting Nicky for the first time even feasible for him. Also there was the the fact that he was barely functioning and he knew it and he simply didn't have anything else to lose.

His wife was gone, he had completely fucked up a major case and he walked out of the Metropolitan Police doubting everything he had ever known about himself. He had absolutely nothing except a giant house that he sat in for weeks at a time, opening the door to only food deliveries and very occasionally Hana.

Luke had very little memory of these weeks. It was as if a sort of slipstream of time muddled the days. He existed only to wake up, shower, get through the day and then be unconscious again, which was really no existence at all. He only slightly remembered the afternoon Hana turned up, how frightened she looked which was so foreign to him.

'I have someone you can speak to.'

He should have been expecting this, but he wasn't. He wasn't offended or surprised, he simply didn't care enough to think about it.

'I don't really think so, Hana. But thank you.'

'Luke, I promise you that this person is really good. A friend from the marines has seen her. My friend was G squadron Luke, tough as anything. Not a therapy person, hates everyone. She swore by this person.'

'Hana, that's good of you. But not now.'

'I've spoken to her. You have an appointment tomorrow at 11am.'

'I'm not going anywhere at 11am tomorrow.'

'Her name is Nicky Bowman. She's only in Highbury. I'll walk you over there. See you tomorrow at 10:15.'

He knew that sometimes there was no arguing with Hana Sawatsky.

————

Luke rang the doorbell and just as she had at 11am that morning ten months ago and many times since, Dr. Nicky Bowman opened her front door and smiled at him.

'Morning,' Luke said.

'Good morning, Luke.'

She turned and began to head upstairs, leaving him to shut the door behind him and wipe his shoes on the mat. He had been so unengaged the first time he walked in this house, blindly following Nicky up the stairs to the room where she saw her patients. But every other time since, Luke has scanned the parts of her ground floor that he can see as he makes his way upstairs — the kitchen, the dining room, part of the living room. What is hanging on the walls? What books are on the shelves? Who is this person that he is letting into his life?

There are many reasons Luke keeps coming back to Nicky to sit in this room in her house, twice a week now, to talk. The moment he opened his mouth, everything came spilling out in a way he hadn't expected and that felt like such a relief. He also liked Nicky — he was 42 and Luke guessed that she would be just the other side of 50. He felt their life experiences may have matched, she was warm and open and clearly very bright. She could also be seriously funny in a biting, shocking way and this pleased him. In another life and another time, he thought they would certainly be friends. And she never flinched or balked or, crucially, was over-sympathetic towards the things that he said. Basically, Hana had been right.

But Luke also knew that one of the reasons he kept coming back here was to try to figure out Nicky Bowman. He had never been in this situation before — to see someone for two hours each week as she sat across from him like a blank slate. What did she do when she wasn't with patients? Did she live in this house alone? Who exactly was she? Even if he had still worked for the Met and had Laura Rowdy at hand to do some digging, it would have been ethically wrong. And besides, Luke thought, what was the fun in that?

So he came to this house in Highbury twice a week and sat in front of Nicky and talked. He was desperate to know more about her, and yet didn't want to know at the same time so he would never be disappointed. Nicky sat across from Luke twice a week and knew he was thinking all of this.

This morning, inevitably, was a little bit different. Luke could see the change come over Nicky's face as he relayed the events of the past few hours.

'This poor woman,' she said. 'You have no idea why she was carrying a piece of paper with your photo on it?'

'No.'

'So what happens next?'

Luke told her how torn he felt. He wanted to leave everything alone and let the police handle it, as he clearly wasn't involved in Chloe Little's death. He couldn't bear the thought of going back to face all of the people he had let down and left behind. But at the same time, he felt excited, like his photograph in the jacket pocket of a dead woman was the first clue in something enormous.

'I'm just not sure that Sadie would want me to do this.'

Nicky was quiet for a moment.

'Luke, your wife is dead. What do *you* want to do?'

EIGHT

What did Luke want to do? He knew, of course. But as he walked away from Nicky's house and through the plane tree lined streets of Highbury back towards his own house, he took a moment to try to convince himself otherwise. Preoccupied with this internal tussle, he didn't see Hana sitting in her car, parked a few houses down. She couldn't help but worry about him and something was not sitting right with this case already. She knew better than to let Luke know she was waiting for him and she let him get far enough away before starting the car and driving towards his house from the opposite direction. She would meet him there.

Hana wouldn't be the only person meeting Luke there. Laura Rowdy had called Hana to let her know that the CCTV from the tube station near to where Chloe Little was found and her phone records were in. And that she would be bringing them over to Luke's house. Laura Rowdy wasn't in the habit of making house calls. In fact, Hana isn't sure she had ever seen Rowdy outside of New Scotland Yard.

Hana pulled the car up to the curb and chuckled to herself

as she looked out the front window. Rowdy may have been the master of decipher and detail, but inconspicuous she was not. She was pacing nervously back and forth on the pavement in front of Luke's house.

'Hi, Rowdy.'

Rowdy looked up and shouted over to Hana.

'He's not here.'

'Yes,' smiled Hana. 'I know. Give it a few minutes.'

Rowdy didn't question how and why Hana knew of Luke's whereabouts.

'So, do I get a hint? You must have found something good to come all the way over here.'

Rowdy looked at Hana and shook her head. Hana wasn't sure what that meant, but guessed that it probably wasn't great.

Fifteen minutes later, with Hana and Rowdy standing making useless small talk, Luke finally appeared around the corner. Hana thought he would have stopped short upon seeing the two of them standing there in front of his house, but he simply smiled and quickened his pace.

'Right, you'd better come in then.'

As they made their way inside, Hana looked over at Rowdy, knowing that she had never been inside Luke's house before. Her eyes widened, but she said nothing and followed them through the hidden portico, its skylight letting the brightness of this autumn day stream into the house.

Luke pulled a bottle of San Pellegrino out of the fridge and handed it to Hana. Pulling three glasses out of one of kitchen cabinets, he nodded towards the kitchen table and the three of them sat down.

'So,' Luke said. 'Let's have it.'

'We have the initial forensic report in,' Rowdy replied. 'Chloe Little died of strangulation. And she was strangled with something interesting. Her neck was covered in minute blue fibres. Dr. Chung said that they looked like they could be a kind of terry cloth material. And, we have some video.'

Rowdy pulled a laptop out of her backpack and inserted the secure internet toggle, the three of them staring at the computer as it booted up and logged on to the Met system.

'Right. First of all, here is the CCTV from Parsons Green tube and the lane from both exits. Rowdy turned the screen to face them and there was Chloe Little, not exiting from the station but rather walking down the street past its entrance.

'She came from the top of the street? From Fulham Road?'

'Looks like it. We will cross reference the time with buses that stop at the top of the lane in each direction, but that is going to take some time.'

'At least we know that she was heading home, not just heading out when she was killed,' Hana said.

'10:23pm. That really isn't very late. No one saw her? Where have they canvassed so far?'

'I understand that the pub, the restaurant across from the station and the grocery store opposite have been done. Staff working that night have been either interviewed or details taken and we are waiting for the relevant CCTV from each of them, in case Chloe went into one of them.'

'Can you back the tape up so we can see it again?' asked Luke.

The three of them leaned in closer to the laptop screen and Rowdy scrolled the cursor back and pressed play one more time. Chloe Little walked past the CCTV camera, looking straight ahead, one hand raised slightly as her thumb was tucked under the strap of her shoulder bag. It was hard to tell what she was wearing as the chilly October evening meant Chloe had on a long coat, belted at the waist.

'She's wearing boots. And presumably tights underneath

that. That looks like a night out that's casual, but with some effort for whoever she was out with,' Hana mused.

'Yes,' Rowdy replied. 'Look.' She pulled another screen up on the laptop and flicked through a couple of crime scene photographs that showed the black tights, expensive looking leather boots and her grey coat had become unloosened by the killer's act, revealing a knee-length black dress.

'She was definitely coming back from somewhere.'

'One more time,' asked Luke, motioning to Rowdy to play the video again.

He didn't lean towards the screen this time, just silently watched Chloe Little walk down Parsons Green Lane. He noted that she was walking quickly, definitely more than a casual stroll. She had wanted to get home. But she wasn't looking at her phone, presumably tucked away in the bag they had not recovered, and she wasn't looking around at her surroundings. Whatever had happened had been a surprise.

'Okay her phone record,' Rowdy said. 'We're obviously just beginning to go through it forensically but there is something interesting already. There were no calls all day - she didn't receive any, or make any. And then between 8:30pm and 8:36pm she made three calls in a row. Two of them lasted for between one and three minutes. The third call had no time stamp, so must not have been answered on the other end.'

'Thank you for bringing all of this over, Rowdy,' Luke said. 'But that's not why you're here.'

Hana looked at him quizzically and then looked over at Rowdy,

'No,' she said quietly. 'I'm sorry, Luke. But Chloe Little has been interviewed by us before.'

Luke and Hana looked at each other, saying nothing.

Rowdy continued. 'I'm sorry that I didn't catch it earlier. It only popped up when I cross-referenced her name with the phone numbers she called last night. One had no record. It must be a pay-as-you-go phone. But the other two are registered to two people we have also interviewed. At the same time we interviewed Chloe Little.'

'Who?'

'Their names are Lucy Bishop and Nigel Quail. They were on the same volunteer committee as Chloe Little.'

'Volunteering for what? I'm not following,' said Hana.

Rowdy took a breath and looked at them both.

'They all worked on a committee with Venetia Wright.'

It was as if time suddenly stood still for Luke, or like he was swimming underwater. He understood what Rowdy had just said, but the words weren't somehow processing through his brain.

Hana was very still.

'Oh god,' she said. 'I interviewed them.'

NINE

FIFTEEN MONTHS EARLIER

L uke and Sadie were still sitting at the kitchen table after dinner when the phone rang.

'It's as if you knew it was going to do that,' Sadie said as she pointed at Luke's phone next to their dirty, empty plates. 'I hate it when you have the phone on the table.'

'Sorry,' Luke smiled and shrugged. He picked it up, seeing that it was his partner's name on the screen.

Sadie saw the name too and stood up to begin clearing away their dishes. She knew that this wasn't a social call.

Luke answered and was quiet for a good minute as he listened to Hana on the other end.

'Okay,' is all he said and then stood up to look for his shoes and coat.

'Everything alright?' Sadie asked.

'I'm sorry, I have to go. This is probably a don't-wait-up kind of evening.'

Sadie waited for her husband to put his shoes on and then buried herself into him, wrapping her arms around his waist, her head against his chest.

'Love you,' muffled out of her.

It was in moments like this where Luke loved her more than he imagined he could. The feeling enveloped him, but he understood that part of it was due to her complete lack of resistance to the nature of his job. The phone calls interrupting their meals, the late nights, the long hours away from her. And sometimes when he was with her, how distracted he became. Sadie knew that this was part of who Luke was, and she somehow, unfathomably, loved him all the more for it.

'Is she collecting you?'

'No. I'm going to meet Hana there. Not too far. Just by Euston Station. See you when I see you.'

'See you when I see you,' she repeated back to him.

———

Luke pulled up to the police cordon, flanked by patrol cars with flashing lights and parked. The heat of the July evening hit him as soon as he began walking toward the scene. For London, it was hotter than usual, the air slightly sticky with humidity and Luke wished he had left his jacket in the car.

Hana had beat him there and was scanning the road in all directions around her, trying to get her bearings.

'Jesus,' she said taking in the sight of Luke as he caught up to her. She pointed to his jacket and raised her eyebrows. 'It's a thousand degrees.'

'It's air conditioned in my house.'

'Of course it is.'

A large area had been cordoned off, spanning close to a quarter of a mile in every direction. Hana had briefed him on the phone, but explained more as they walked towards the scene.

'I thought that maybe the road system of one-way traffic around here forced the cordon to be so large, but it's not that. They really want to get this guy. It's possible that he hasn't gone far. Officers are fanned out looking, everyone has been called in.'

'Do they have an ID on the victim?'

'Yes, her name is Venetia Wright. Does that ring a bell?'

'No,' Luke shook his head. 'Should it?'

'Extremely wealthy, apparently. The name isn't familiar to me, but I thought maybe she ran in similar circles to Sadie and you had come across her or something.'

'My wife may be wealthy, Hana, but that doesn't mean she knows all rich people.'

'Sorry, I know. Not what I meant to say.'

Hana suddenly felt stupid. Why would Luke know who this was, anymore than she would? Or Sadie for that matter?

The flash of the medical examiner's camera drew their attention to the scene in front of them.

'Good evening, Wiley. Evening Sawatsky,' she said.

'Can we take a look? Has this area been cleared?'

'Yes, come on over,' Dr. Chung said. Chung was, thought Luke, the perfect medical examiner. Meticulous, thorough, smart, and straight shooting. He liked her immensely.

'Where did they pull you from this fine, sweltering evening?' Luke asked her.

'I was in the lab, actually. Nice to get some fresh air.'

Hana looked at Luke and shook her head. That comment should have been funny in the stinking hot weather they were all standing in, but Chung didn't really have a sense of humour.

The trail of blood was smeared on the pavement and had

eventually pooled underneath the body, seeping down to the left where the ground was uneven.

'It would have been a quick death, but not instant. She dragged herself a few feet,' Chung said.

'Shit,' said Hana. 'What else?'

'Two stab wounds. Not a big blade from the entrance wounds here....and here. But something that could do some damage. Switchblade, small hunting knife, something like that.' Chung pointed to the victim's back, her silk blouse stuck to her body not from sweat, but by dried blood.

'First impressions?' Luke asked.

Chung stood up and removed her face mask.

'Look, I'm never going to rule anything out at this point. Could it be random? Sure. But this feels slightly more personal, or at least angrier, to me. Two quick, decisive movements and this poor woman is dead.'

'How was she ID'd so quickly?' asked Luke. 'Where is the first responder?'

'I'll get him for you. I'm going to have the coroner move her now as I'm all done here. See you in the lab later. I can give you the full report in the morning.'

Chung strode off and Luke and Hana surveyed their surroundings. It was darker than it should have been for the twilight sky of a July late evening in London. They were in a small alley with no overhead lamps that ran between two small streets. On one side was a brick wall that would have backed onto the gardens of the houses one street over — too high to easily scale. On the other side were two disused premises — once upon a time a small restaurant and a shop, but they looked like they had been empty for some time. CCTV was not going to help them here.

The first responding officer approached them.

'Sir. DS Sawatsky,' he nodded.

The young officer took them through it. A customer

coming out of the cocktail bar at one end of the alley discovered the body and called an ambulance.

'Was she deceased when you arrived?' Hana asked.

'Yes. Medical crew had worked on her but I arrived within a couple of minutes and when they called it, I secured everything.'

'Well done,' Luke said. 'And the ID?'

'In her pocket, Sir. There was no bag or anything with her, so I did check. In her trouser pocket was a credit card with her name on it.'

'Nothing else with her at all?'

'No, Sir. Once the scene was secured, I checked in with the cocktail bar and she had come from there. She must have just left.'

Luke and Hana thanked the officer and watched as the coroner team gently lifted the body of Venetia Wright up and onto a stretcher, its body bag lined and open for her.

'One moment, please,' Luke said and he and Hana took a look at her, now that she was facing up.

Venetia Wright was probably in her late forties, dressed simply in jeans and a black silk blouse. No watch or jewelry apart from tiny, exquisite diamond studs. Her left ear had two of them.

'Well, let's find out what she was doing here. Shall we?'

Luke pointed down the alley towards the bar and Hana stepped in front of him, squeezing past the forensics team who were on their hands and knees, scouring for anything useful.

When they got to the end of the alley, they were confused.

'Was it at the other end, do you think?' Hana asked.

The street they were standing on was just a row of residential mews houses. It was a pretty street, blocked at each end by traffic calming flower beds, it was pedestrian and cycle only, making it seem very quiet.

'Detectives?'

Hana and Luke turned around to see a door of one of the houses open, a police officer standing inside.

'It's in here.'

To their surprise, this little mews house was actually a cocktail bar, all wood panelled walls, roaring fireplace at the back and an upright piano in the corner, no pianist but rather a couple sitting on the bench sipping from tumblers, the keyboard cover holding candles and coasters.

'I've taken all names and details, Sir,' said the officer. 'But this is a private members club, so everyone in here is very easy to track down. Strict admission and all that.'

Luke couldn't help but make a mental note to find out what on earth this place was and how he could become a member here. Sadie would absolutely love it.

'The manager is just in the back. Would you like to follow me, Sir.'

Luke and Hana took it all in as they weaved through the ground floor of this little house, each room with comfortable furniture, small tables glittering with glasses, what was once the kitchen now a long mahogany topped bar, the bartender behind it peeling perfectly uniform strips of orange peel. He smiled at them as they walked past.

The manager was chatting with guests in the backroom of the house and politely stepped away to greet them.

'Detectives, welcome. Please won't you follow me?'

He continued into the house where a staircase led to the second floor and the three of them headed upstairs. The room was one large space, a desk and filing cabinets on one side and a seating area on the other.

'Can I get you anything? I can call down?'

'No, that's fine,' Hana said.

'I'm Detective Chief Inspector Wiley and this is Detective Sergeant Sawatsky. Could you tell us a little bit about this bar? I understand it's members only?'

The manager who had been all smiles, floating around his guests with ease just a moment ago suddenly looked ashen faced and sunk into his chair slightly.

'Yes, of course. We are a members-only bar, part of the Ambrose Club Group. We've been open here for about two years.'

'The Ambrose is the private member club in Soho?' Hana said.

'Yes, that's right. With another club in Mayfair, just off Portland Place, and then this cocktail bar. I'm sorry, but I can't believe what has happened. Your officer told me. I didn't know what to do. He said I didn't need to close down for the night, which I was relieved about, but I feel quite shaken.'

'Did you know Venetia Wright?' asked Luke.

'Oh yes. I mean, not well, or that personally. But she came in here often enough and she was so nice. You sometimes get members who aren't so nice — entitled, you know? But Venetia was always so friendly and the staff liked her.'

'How often did she come in here?'

'Once or twice a month, maybe.'

Hana felt sorry for the manager, probably picturing what happened to Venetia just down the street.

'Who was she with when she was here?'

'Friends, mostly. Women friends. That's who she was with tonight. They'd been in before, maybe last month.'

'What was their mood like? Did everything seem normal?'

The manager nodded. 'Totally normal. They both had two dirty vodka martinis each, were laughing and relaxed. Everything was fine.'

'Did she ever come in here with a man?' asked Luke.

'Oh yes. Her husband.'

'And what is he like?' prodded Hana.

'I don't really know him. Nice enough. Quiet, I guess.'

'Is he also a member here?'

'No. Actually, he's not.'

Hana leaned forward. 'How are you so sure?'

'Because when you enter the bar, I bring over a screen that scans your membership card. If you're not a member, the member you are accompanying can register you ahead of time by email or calling, or if they just turn up with a non-member then we physically sign them into our guestbook.'

'Old fashioned,' mused Hana.

'Well, it's a members club. It's how it works. I know that Venetia's husband is definitely not a member.'

'And the woman Venetia was drinking with here this evening?'

'She's a member,' the manager said.

'We're going to need those details,' said Luke as he stood up.

TEN

The sight of the police cars parked in front of Chloe's house had made Lucy feel sick to her stomach. It was a shock to see them there, filling the street she had walked down so many times on her way to visit Chloe. Nights in with bottles of good wine and gossipy conversation. It was so much more comfortable than her own house and she often offered to cook when she came over. Chloe's kitchen had everything you could possibly want — the electronic measuring scales and Creuset pans, silicone spatulas in different colours.

'You always cook the most amazing things, Luce,' Chloe often said. What Chloe didn't know is that Lucy would research recipes that she would love to cook for herself — dishes that featured spices like zatar and fenugreek and star anise. Things that Lucy would never have in her own kitchen cupboards — even if she splurged to buy them, they would be used once or twice and then left to turn stale. It seemed like such a waste. But she knew that Chloe would have them and wouldn't worry about their expiry date. Chloe was the kind of person who would just buy the same spices all over again if they were past their best. She always felt that she was worth having good things that made life feel full. Lucy loved that about her.

Her hands were shaking as she called Michael. When he didn't answer, she put her phone away and decided to walk the rest of the way home instead of taking the tube a few stops east. She had to think.

By the time she reached her flat she knew that she only had one option. She really didn't feel like it. She picked up her phone and scrolled through her contacts until she found his name. She pressed it, took a breath and placed the phone to her ear. It rang and rang and she felt a brief moment of irritation that she was going to get his voice mail, which ordinarily would have been just fine with her.

'Lucy?'

'Hi Nigel. Yes. I'm sorry to bother you again but we really need to speak.'

'Is this about Chloe?'

'Yes,' Lucy said. 'It's just that I wandered over to her house just now and...'

Nigel cut her off.

'Lucy.'

'What?'

'Chloe is dead.'

Lucy opened her mouth but her breath caught and what came out was a small moan.

'I'm sorry Lucy, but the police are here. I have to go.'

The phone went dead in Lucy's hand. She held it there anyway, with the terrible realization that very soon the police would know that the she was the last person Chloe called.

———

Except that Lucy was not the last person Chloe called. The phone records Rowdy pulled up showed that the last person Chloe called the previous evening before she was killed was Nigel and that is why Detective Inspector Hackett and his partner Detective Smith knocked on his door ten minutes before.

Nigel let them inside, ushering them in quickly.

'I'm sorry,' he said. 'Nosey neighbours. Don't want anyone talking. What is this about?'

The three men were still standing in the front hall when Hackett informed Nigel that Chloe Little was dead. Nigel seemed to sway on the spot, Hackett wondering if the man might be about to faint. He looked down at the carpet and quietly told the detectives that they had better come in and sit down.

Hackett and Smith looked around at the messy living room, remnants of breakfast on dishes still sitting on the coffee table. Newspaper pages all folded the same way with crossword puzzles and sudokus, mostly empty were piled on one side of the couch and Nigel sat down on the other.

'What happened?' he asked. His hands were visibly shaking.

'I'm afraid she was killed last night. It looks like she was attacked while she was on her way home. Did you speak with her yesterday? Do you know where she was yesterday evening?'

'No, I'm sorry.'

'Where was she calling you from?'

'She didn't say, I'm afraid.'

Hackett leaned forward. 'And what was the content of your conversation?'

As if in response to Hackett's gesture, Nigel leaned forward as well. 'Chloe wanted to do something with me next week. Spend some time together. She suggested that we have dinner, just the two of us.'

'She called you last night to ask you for dinner?' Smith asked.

'Yes,' Nigel beamed. 'That's right. She and I had, what would you call it, a *connection* and she liked to spend time with me. And I with her, of course. We hadn't had the opportunity for some one on one time lately and she wanted to fix that.'

'When did you plan to have dinner?'

'We didn't set a firm time. Just sometime next week.'

'And you don't know where she was calling from, or why she called you at nine o'clock last night to ask you for dinner?'

'No.' Nigel bristled slightly. 'Why wouldn't she call me last night? I can't help that she was thinking about me.'

It was at this moment that Nigel's phone began to ring. Nigel and the detectives looked over at the screen, all of them seeing the name that flashed up at the same time. Hackett and Smith looked at each other.

Completely missing the look at passed between the detectives, Nigel picked up the phone and answered it. He would be the one to tell the others what had happened.

————

The previous evening Nigel Quail had been upstairs in his den, furiously typing way between three different online forums. There was so much he had to say. In the comment section of a particularly divisive news article, he was debating the recent behaviour of a politician and his possibly shady fundraising, in another chat group he was urging a woman who had spent the past couple of months posting about her boyfriend and their difficulties to think twice about moving in together, and in the third online forum where an anonymous poster wondered if he had been right to call the council about a hedge that had been planted too close to his property line, Nigel strenuously agreed with him.

His mobile was next to him on the desk when it rang just after nine o'clock. Chloe's name flashed onto the screen and Nigel felt a small thrill flutter through him. He waited a beat before pressing the answer button. As delighted as he was to be receiving the call, there had been the difficult chat between them which had upset him, and that needed to be recognized by Chloe so Nigel felt she could wait just a moment.

'Hello?'

He would make her think that he did not have her name saved into his contact list.

'Oh, hello Chloe,' he replied. 'What are you up to? I'm just in the middle of something here but I have a moment.'

What followed was not what Nigel expected. It was a short phone call and he sat in his den, his phone still in his hand, stunned at what Chloe had said. He wished that he had hung up on her. Angry at himself that he had not done so, had not been quick enough to react, he abandoned all three of his internet posts, shut down his computer and went downstairs to get his coat. He needed to get out of the house and deal with this.

ELEVEN

Hackett excused himself from the interview between Smith and Nigel Quail and stepped into the hall-way. He scrolled through his phone contacts until he found the name he needed and pressed the call button.

Hana was still sitting at Luke's kitchen table, Rowdy having left them to ponder the disconcerting news she had come over to deliver, when she answered.

'Oh shit. Yes, okay, on our way now. Text the address.' She hung up and told Luke to grab his keys and his coat because they had to go.

'What's up?'

'Hackett and Smith are interviewing Nigel Quail right now. Lucy Bishop called in the middle of it and the guy told her that Chloe was dead. We have to get to her now.'

Hana was almost out of the kitchen but Luke had not yet moved from the table.

'Luke, we can keep talking on the way.'

He took a deep breath, followed her out the door and into the car.

Hana looked over at Luke in the passenger seat and could tell that he was deep in thought about the old case. She knew they were going to have to revisit it at some point. Hana said a silent prayer to herself that he would be okay, while desperately wishing that this wasn't happening.

'At the beginning of the Venetia Wright case, when we dealt with her at the scene, and then began to track everyone down, did you have an inkling of what was ahead?' Hana asked.

Luke shook his head. 'Absolutely no idea.'

'Yeah, me too. Normal day, sad case, but nothing unusual.'

'Hana,' Luke said. 'If you are trying to make me feel better here you're doing a really shit job.'

Hana clenched her jaw, focusing on the road. She had also been the one to drive them fifteen months ago to the house of Maggie Joseph — the friend who had been drinking with Venetia Wright in the members only cocktail bar.

So many years of turning up at the door of grieving people did not make these visits feel routine or any easier. They had arrived just before midnight and Maggie was already asleep. It was her husband who had opened the door and even though there were two detectives turning up at their door at that hour, Luke and Hana could tell once they were all seated in the living room that the two people in front of them had no idea what they were about to be told.

Maggie went into a state of deep shock. Her husband was very quiet. Luke knew he was silently thanking his gods that the deceased was not his own wife. He grasped Maggie's hand and was the one to ask what had happened.

Maggie was in disbelief and her words came out in a stammer as she tried to speak.

'But...how...could this happen? I....was....just with her.'

Luke knew to let Hana lead this conversation. They did not have much time to waste here and she would be able to get more information out of the poor woman.

'Did Venetia say anything at all tonight that could have indicated she thought was in danger?'

'No. Not at all. She was in a great mood. We had a really nice time.' Tears ran down Maggie's face.

'In a better mood that usual, would you say?'

Maggie shook her head. 'No, she was always like that. Always positive. Oh god...' The emotion began to move through her body and Maggie began to sob.

Her husband gripped Maggie's hand tighter. 'I just cannot believe this has happened,' he said.

Hana kept going. 'Do you remember what she was wearing tonight?'

'Um, jeans and a black shirt, I think.'

'Was she wearing jewelry?' Hana asked.

Maggie paused. 'I don't remember specifically. But she wasn't really a jewelry person. She always wore her watch. Sometimes a bracelet. She may have been wearing it tonight. I'm not sure.'

'Can you describe them?'

'The bracelet was a silver bangle that had a few small diamonds embedded in it. It was a gift from her husband. The watch was a Patek Philippe.'

Luke raised his eyebrows and the husband asked what they were all thinking.

'Was this a robbery?'

'We're not sure,' Luke said. 'My officers have gone to the Wright residence and no one is there. Do you know where Venetia's husband is?'

'He's away on business. I think he left earlier today,' Maggie said.

Maggie wasn't sure where he had gone exactly, but Marcus

Wright was a brand consultant and had a few employees that worked in Glasgow, so he may be in Scotland.

'And the marriage?'

'Oh good,' Maggie said. 'He absolutely adores her. Oh god, Marcus will be devastated. Just devastated.'

The detectives had the basics and were getting ready to leave this poor couple, who now wouldn't get a minute of sleep.

'One last thing,' Luke said. 'We didn't recover a phone at the scene. Did Venetia have one with her tonight, or a bag? We didn't find a bag with her either.'

'No. Neither. But she never did. Venetia was simple — always carried just a card, maybe a lipgloss. She wasn't a fussy or particular person. And she always said that mobile phones had ruined how we spend our time. She was adamant that just because her phone moved around with her, it didn't mean that she was reachable all the time. She treated it like a landline, really. If she was home, she'd answer it. So eventually, she just stopped bringing it out with her if it wasn't necessary. And I know she didn't have it with her because I was running a bit late and tried calling but she didn't answer.'

The other person who wasn't answering his phone that evening was Marcus Wright. Rowdy had pulled up the number and Luke called him repeatedly but it went straight to voice mail. Rowdy couldn't use GSM to find him, meaning his phone was not emitting a signal to any nearby antenna mast. It was firmly turned off.

'Or he's dumped it,' Hana said.

A brutally murdered woman, a distraught best friend and a missing husband. The recipe for a easy to assemble meal, but Luke and Hana had no idea how complicated the ingredients would turn out to be.

Twelve

As Hana and Luke's car weaved through London traffic towards Earl's Court and the home of Lucy Bishop, they were both deep in thought. Hana needed to say it and felt nervous. She never felt nervous.

'Luke, look. I'm really sorry that I didn't pick up on the name earlier. Chloe Little. That I had interviewed her.'

'There's no need to be sorry,' Luke replied. 'Why would that name stick out to you? It was fifteen months ago.'

'I know. But if you had interviewed her, I doubt you would have forgotten the name.'

'Don't be ridiculous, Hana. I don't have perfect recall.'

Hana didn't say anything but she was thinking to herself, *well, you kind of do.*

The light in front of them turned red and Hana applied the brakes. She turned to Luke and put her hand gently on his arm.

'I know. Look, Luke, your photo was found on a murdered woman last night so shall we get into it?'

Luke couldn't help but laugh quietly.

'Okay, go ahead. What do you remember about Chloe Little?'

'Honestly?' Hana said. 'Not a hell of a lot. I just remember that there were four of them. They all came into the station together and I think I interviewed them in pairs. It was really just fact finding as they all had very clear alibis on the night Venetia was killed. They were never suspects. I do remember thinking that they didn't need to be separated for questioning.'

'And they worked with Venetia?'

'Sort of. More volunteering.'

Venetia Wright was wealthy. Top one percent kind of wealthy and it was family money that had been inherited. At the time, Luke and Hana had delved deep into her background looking for any kind of clue or motivation as the weeks dragged on and there was no strong suspect, only a couple of men pulled in for questioning who had been picked up on CCTV around the area she was killed. Her watch and bracelet had never surfaced — no leads as to a theft. No leads anywhere and the Met was under tremendous pressure to arrest someone.

Venetia had grown up in a safe, nurturing household. Both of her parents had died while she was in her thirties — both cancer — and Venetia had risen to the occasion. The boards her parents sat on welcomed her, the money was donated to various causes as it had always been, and her favourite charity took up a large chunk of her time.

The charity was an education fund for school aged girls in various parts of India. When her second parent had died, Venetia spent three months travelling there, the typical search for meaning in a difficult time, and there she had found a new way to spend her inherited money that gave her huge purpose.

'And that's where Chloe Little and the rest of them came in,' Hana said.

'They were volunteers for the charity?'

'Yes. They were volunteers in that they weren't paid for their work, but Venetia had set up the charity so they were all non-executive directors of it.'

'Meaning what exactly?'

'Meaning that I remember all four of them talking about how rewarding they found working there and how wonderful Venetia was to give them autonomy. They were all clearly distressed by her death. Venetia oversaw everything but she trusted these four people to look after everything.'

'And you feel this is important to point out now. Why?'

Hana took a moment to answer. She wished that she and Luke weren't being dragged back into an old case that both of them would frankly never like to think about again. But this back and forth conversation — the way they questioned each other, how they sometimes finished each other's sentences because they were figuring out that whatever was in front of them didn't quite make sense — this is how it was meant to be with them. It felt good.

'Because Chloe Little was found murdered in the early evening, heading home. Just like Venetia. She had a photograph of you in her pocket. The last person she called was one of the four directors of Venetia's charity and while the police are questioning him, he gets a call from the third member of this merry band of charity workers.'

'Which means there is one more question,' said Luke. 'Where's the fourth?'

———

Michael finally found his phone at lunchtime. He had wandered out to his home office in the garden and was upset to find the door unlocked. His computer was still sitting on his desk, and so was his phone. Who had last been in here?

One of his sons, most likely, or had he come in late last night and in his drunken state not remembered? Lottie generally refused to come down here, irritated by how much time he spent at the edge of the property seemingly ignoring her.

When Michael picked up the phone, his stomach flipped. Twenty seven missed calls. Three voicemails.

He quickly pressed the button to call his voicemail. He knew who this would be, waiting for her voice at the other end. Accusatory, angry, upset. Possibly pleading.

But it wasn't her. It was Nigel. Polite, slightly strange Nigel asking if he could please call him at his convenience. He deleted the message.

The next one was a woman as he had expected, but not the right one. It was Lucy. She was also asking Michael to call her. The third was Lucy calling again. This time, she sounded angry. She had clearly spoken to Chloe. Michael looked at the phone log and each of them had called multiple times. The last call was Lucy's final voicemail, just after midnight. Thank god his phone was out here.

He would wait to call them back. He'd have a quiet weekend with Lottie and try to get back on track. He would put his irritations behind him and look at his good life and his lovely family and focus on the future. It was like waking in the night when all your anxieties felt worse — would his career finally move to the next level or was he stuck there? Why did his kids spend so much time online? Would they be okay? Was he still in love with his wife?

All of this would be fine. He would take the weekend to relax and think about everything on Monday. Nigel and Lucy could wait.

———

It was as if Lucy was expecting Luke and Hana. She had opened the door before they were even out of the car.

'I'm Detective Chief Inspector Wiley,' Luke said, for the first time in over a year. The words flew out of his mouth without hesitation. He hesitated for a moment, realizing that he probably shouldn't have introduced himself this way.

'And I believe you have previously met Detective Sergeant Sawatsky?'

Lucy nodded. 'Please come in.'

There wasn't much room inside the small flat and although seemingly waiting for the detectives to turn up, Lucy just stood there, not moving any further inside.

'We understand that you have been told that Chloe Little has been found dead?'

Lucy nodded again. 'Yes, I called Nigel and he told me. I figured you would be coming here too. I spoke to her last night.'

'Would you mind if we sat down?' Hana asked.

'I'm sorry. Yes, of course.' Lucy looked flustered and tugged at her shirt sleeves as she led the detectives into the first room a few feet from the front door where they had been standing. There was barely room for all of them to be seated.

'What time did Chloe call you?'

Lucy swallowed and wondered why they were asking this. Surely they already knew from Chloe's phone log.

'Around nine, I guess?'

'And what was she calling for?'

'She'd been on a date and he hadn't shown up.'

'Well, that's not very nice. Chloe was stood up?' Hana asked.

'She...she wasn't sure,' Lucy said. 'She wondered if she had been, or if it had been some sort of misunderstanding about the time or whatever.'

'Who was she meeting?'

'I don't know.'

Luke smiled at her and Lucy suddenly felt nervous.

'You don't know who she was meeting?'

'No,' Lucy said. 'She didn't say. I mean, she said it was another first date and if it went well she would fill me in when we next saw each other. That's what she was calling me about. To see if I was free tomorrow to have lunch.'

Hana suddenly stood up and walked over to the IKEA set of bookshelves that leaned against the opposite wall. She picked up a framed photograph and held it up.

'This is you and Chloe,' she said.

'Yes, that's right.'

'Chloe has the same photograph framed in her house.'

Lucy swallowed. They had already been in Chloe's house.

'Yes, she had the photograph framed and gave it to me for Christmas a couple of years ago.'

Hana couldn't remember the genesis of this friendship, or more likely it had never come up during the Venetia Wright case as they had been otherwise occupied.

'Remind me how you met Chloe? Was it on Venetia Wright's charity committee?'

'Before that,' said Lucy. 'We met in India when we were both travelling through there. We met Venetia at the same time. That's how we got involved in her charity.'

'And the others? On the committee? How did they get involved?'

'I'm not sure about Nigel. He does a lot of volunteering and I think he came across the charity through another one and got involved that way. Michael is a dad at the school where I teach. One of his sons is a pupil and the charity was looking for someone with financial experience, so I asked him.'

'He works in finance,' said Luke.

'Yes.'

'Have you spoken to him today?'

'Uh, no. No, I haven't.'

Lucy felt brave for a moment and thought she should assert herself with these two detectives asking her so many questions while sitting in her living room.

'Why do you ask, detective?'

'I'm wondering why you called Nigel this morning, and not Michael. And why exactly did you call Nigel?'

Lucy's bravery fell away and she shifted in her place on the sofa. Why were they asking so many questions about the committee? Was it possible that they knew what they were all hiding?

'I couldn't remember if we were all meeting this week, so I rang Nigel to find out.'

'Why ring him? Why not send a text or an email?' asked Hana.

Lucy shrugged her shoulders. 'I feel a bit sorry for Nigel. He seems like a lonely guy and I always think it's nice to reach out, to give him a call when he's probably not going to be speaking to anyone else all weekend.'

When Lucy finally shut the door behind the detectives as they walked back to their car, Lucy smiled to herself. Technically, nothing she had said to them was a lie. It was much easier this way.

THIRTEEN

'What do you think?' Hana said, when they sat back down in her car. 'Was she lying?'

'There's always a lie somewhere,' Luke replied. 'It will reveal itself sooner or later.'

They hadn't questioned her for long, but long enough to ascertain that the slightly generic answers Lucy gave them meant that something wasn't adding up.

Hana had been surprised that Luke had asked Lucy if she and the other committee members ever discussed Venetia's murder. What had he been hoping she was going to say? Was Luke thinking Lucy was going to reveal that Chloe was, in fact, obsessed with the murder of her former colleague and couldn't let it go? Lucy had fobbed off these questions with short, deflecting answers. They were no closer to finding out why Chloe was carrying a photograph of Luke in her coat pocket.

'You know that O'Donnell is going to be furious when he finds out you came to this interview with me.'

'Oh, I know.'

'Hackett was good to tip us off and get us over there. I'm

sure O'Donnell will understand that. Or at least let's hope so. Otherwise an ex-DCI all over this interview isn't going to go down that well.'

Luke chortled. 'Well, shall we find out?'

'Are you sure? I can head back to the Yard on my own.'

'Like I have anything else to do.'

———

Walking back into Scotland Yard for the second time in one day was not something Luke ever thought he would do again. He hated that it felt so comfortable.

Hana was right — O'Donnell had hit the roof. He pounced on them both as soon as they stepped off the elevator.

'Get in here!' he shouted, turning the heads of every single person on the Serious Crime Command desk.

'Can't believe I'm getting detention again,' Luke said. 'I hate staying after school.'

Hana suppressed a laugh and they dutifully followed O'Donnell into his office.

'Shut the goddamn door,' O'Donnell growled at them.

'Look, Stephen. I'm sure you can appreciate this rather unique circumstance...'

'Do not talk, Wiley! I've had absolutely enough of you. You are no longer Detective Chief Inspector Wiley, you are no longer a member of the Metropolitan Police Force. You are nothing!'

O'Donnell's outburst seemed to shock all three of them into silence. Luke felt his anger rising and began to breathe in through his nose and out through his mouth. This was a common emotion over the past year and Nicky Bowman had taught him this simple technique. He was bemused that it worked, but it did.

Luke didn't know what was going to foster the better outcome here — to sit in a war of silent attrition until O'Donnell gave up, or to argue his case. He opted for the latter, slightly nervous of what Hana was going to do in the meantime. She was the one with the career to worry about. His no longer mattered.

'A woman has been murdered. She had a photograph of me in her pocket. Assuming I am not a suspect as you haven't arrested me yet, I think this possibly warrants a bit of leeway here. I would like to formally ask to be temporarily reinstated.'

O'Donnell snorted. 'Absolutely not.'

'Fine,' Luke said. 'Then I'd like to speak to Marina.'

'Oh be my bloody guest,' O'Donnell looked incredulous at this point. He waved his arm towards the door.

Hana took this moment to ease out of her chair and opened the door to escape. Luke stood up to join her. O'Donnell glared at them both.

'Well, this is a bit of a risk, don't you think?' asked Hana.

'Honestly, what have I got to lose here? I'll pop upstairs and see if she's in.'

'Right. Good luck.'

Luke walked back towards the elevators and punched the button. He clearly remembered the last time he saw Marina Scott-Carson. She had come to Sadie's funeral, which had been a bit of a surprise and a lovely gesture. She had also made a point of being seen at the funeral by all the right people, ever the operator. But she was the boss and there was a reason she had got to the status not many women in their line of work achieved.

The elevator whisked Luke four floors up to the top level of the building. They opened and standing right in front of the elevator door was Marina Scott-Carson. She was smiling, which was unusual, but her dyed blonde hair as striking as ever.

'Commissioner,' Luke said. 'Hello. I was just coming to see if you had a moment for a quick word.'

'Did you think I'm just coincidentally waiting for you at the elevator, Wiley? O'Donnell rang up.'

'Right,' Luke said. He extended his arm to prevent the elevator door from closing on him and stepped out next to Scott-Carson.

'You'd better follow me.'

Marina Scott-Carson had a grand office that looked more like a formal drawing room than a sterile office cubicle. Luke wouldn't have been surprised to see a roaring fireplace and a butler standing in the corner. He waited to ask to be seated. Scott-Carson took her time in asking him.

'I understand that you have asked for a temporary re-instatement to your former position.' She shuffled through the large piles of papers on her desk, not looking at Luke.

'Yes, that's right. I'm not sure if O'Donnell has explained the specific circumstances regarding my request.'

'And how are you doing, Wiley?'

Luke paused and bit the inside of his cheek.

'Not great, really.'

Scott-Carson finally looked up at him and removed her tortoiseshell reading glasses.

'Well, that's comforting.'

They stared at each other.

'Look, Wiley,' she tossed her glasses onto the desk in front of her. 'A particularly difficult request, don't you think? We have another murdered woman, a photograph of the detective who blew the last major murder case we had in her pocket, and this detective is now asking me to come back to work. And to be put on this case, I assume?'

Luke nodded. 'Yeah, it does look a bit shit, doesn't it?'

'How do I know that what happened before isn't about to happen again?'

Luke considered her question. 'Well, you don't really. You know that I always accepted responsibility for what happened. It's one of the reasons I left.'

Scott-Carson leaned back in her chair and pursed her lips.

'You got too close, Wiley. You got lost in it. You made a major mistake. Far, far too close.'

Luke looked down at his hands, the defeat about to be handed to him almost too much to bear. Scott-Carson put her reading glasses back on and opened the file folder on the top of the teetering pile next to her.

'It's also what makes you human, Wiley. Unlike the rest of the robots on floor seven.' She paused. 'Nothing is unforgivable. Your new ID pass will be ready in an hour.'

Luke's jaw dropped. He had never before felt such a wave of admiration for Marina Scott-Carson. Or this amount of gratitude. He thanked her and stood up to leave.

'Oh, one more thing Wiley. I suggest you bypass O'Donnell on your way out. I'll handle him.'

Fourteen

Figuring out where the photograph of Luke Wiley, found inside the coat pocket of Chloe Little, came from was easy in the end. A search for 'Detective Inspector Luke Wiley' in Google Image brought it up instantly. It had been taken a couple of years earlier during a talk Luke had given to criminology students at Kings College London.

'She clearly was using this to spot you somewhere,' Hana said. 'Like she wanted to pick you out of a line up or something.'

Hana was stretched out on the sofa in Luke's living room. It had been a long day, the kind of working hours that Luke was no longer used to and he was tired. Luke tapped the glass teapot full of green tea leaves that he had brought in on a tray and looked at his watch. The gas fireplace was flickering to life across the room, having automatically turned itself on when the thermostat read that it was cool enough to do so.

'Does that ever freak you out?' Hana asked.

'Used to it. So, Chloe Little was looking for me. Why? To tell me something? But what was specific about Friday night?'

'Possibly nothing. Do you know how often I remove the stuff I have shoved in my coat pockets? Not that often. What were your movements over the past week?'

Luke had to think. His days had seemed so full with Sadie and now he existed in a sort of timeless universe. He had never been someone who stuck to a routine, but his wife loved them. She found comfort in the daily tasks she created for herself after she had sold her business and suddenly had more time in her day than she knew what to do with. When Luke found himself in the same position, he tried to do the same. Probably not as successfully, but he tried.

He remembered telling Nicky about his attempts to formulate a schedule to his days which otherwise seemed to exist in free fall. How he would set the alarm, roast his coffee beans, do the New York Times puzzles first — they had been Sadie's favourites — go for a run. He tried to stretch out the morning with these tasks because otherwise the day felt unbearably long. Nicky had been pleased, impressed almost, and Luke felt embarrassed to feel proud about scoring marks with his therapist. Sadie would have thought that was charming and he had to shut those kinds of thoughts down, like snapping shut a thick book or turning off a running tap, otherwise his despair would overwhelm him. Sometimes it did anyway.

'Honestly Hana, it was kind of a quiet week.'

'Did you go to yoga?'

'Yes,' Luke replied. 'Both Tuesday and Thursday actually.'

'Which classes? Sadie's usual ones or the evening sessions?' Sadie had been a yoga devotee for many years, and it was in these classes that she met Hana. And then wine after the classes is where they became fast friends.

'We can check the CCTV nearby for the whole day - in case Chloe was following you.'

Luke couldn't help but shiver. Cases didn't affect him in

this way, he didn't usually feel threatened or unnerved, but then again he never usually played such a role and for a reason that couldn't be good.

Hana poured herself a cup of tea and then one for Luke. She added a dash of hot water that Luke had put on the tray just for her.

'What about The Robson?'

'Didn't go.'

'Any reason?'

'I went to yoga instead.'

What Luke didn't say to Hana was that sometimes going to The Robson made him sadder than it was possible to bear.

———

Luke had quickly learned that Sadie had absolutely no problem revealing to him the rather peculiar life she lived. The first time Luke walked into her house on that third date, he made some banal comment about how lovely it was, and then purposely said nothing. He stayed over that night and in the morning, he felt ridiculous.

How could he not say anything? The house was incredible, unlike anything he had ever seen. And it must have cost an absolute fortune. The previous evening, Sadie had accepted the compliment by explaining in great detail how she had a design in her head about what the house should look like once the two buildings were knocked together and how the architects had been gracious in letting her assist in so many aspects of its design and construction.

She pointed out hinges, and expanded bespoke door frames and hammered bronze transition strips between the beautiful oak hardwood and the polished cement that had underfloor heating. Luke had nodded along, more in awe with the capabilities of this woman and her bizarre extensive knowledge of house renovation, than with the design itself.

She had mentioned on their first date that she worked in tech and had sold her small company when she was thirty.

'It has left me a lot of time,' Sadie had said.

He felt embarrassed now to ask her exactly what she did and didn't want to ask too many questions. Instead, that next morning he asked if he could take her out again, anywhere in London that was her favourite spot.

'Oh,' she said. 'That's easy. The Robson, Thursday night.'

Right, Luke had thought to himself. He knew of The Robson, of course, but had never set foot in there himself. It was considered by most to be one of the most exclusive hotels in London, right in the heart of Mayfair. Built at the opening of the twentieth century, it was a classic in Art Deco architecture, with five star service, and prices to match.

'I like the lobby bar. Not the dining room. You'll need to make a reservation.'

'Sounds good,' Luke had said.

It was in this lobby bar, its private corners and glass topped tables, its perfect lighting and lack of cocktail menu because you just ordered whatever you wanted, that Sadie began to tell her story.

'You're probably wondering why I wanted to come here.'

'It's a great spot, I can see why you wanted to go for drinks here.'

Sadie smiled at him and gently touched his hand, which was holding a stiff Hendricks and tonic.

'Actually, it's more than that. My parents used to come here when I was a little girl. I'm not really sure why. It was less celebrity, more old school London back then. And they always used to bring me. We used to have dinner together in this bar, and I ignored them mostly. I usually brought a book and just read.'

Luke could picture it perfectly. He listened, captivated by this strange, wonderful woman sitting across from him. Sadie explained that her loss when they died was difficult, and they died before she had made a success of her small tech company, and before she sold it for thirty million pounds.

Luke had spluttered his drink, grabbing a cocktail napkin and pressing it to his lips. Sadie laughed, this perfect laugh and took a deep breath.

'Thank you for that honest reaction. I never know how to tell people. Well, I don't ever tell people, but I think that maybe you are not people.'

Luke would always remember this moment. A moment where two people would meet and fall into each others' lives like the final missing piece of a jigsaw puzzle. And that crucially, in that moment, the other person felt the exact same way. Puzzle complete.

'I hadn't come to The Robson in years. But when I sold my company, I felt, I don't know....bereft...because my parents didn't see what I was able to do. I brought myself here, alone, and had dinner. And it was sort of fabulous?' She said this as a question, like she couldn't quite believe it.

'So this is what I often do on a Thursday night. You see the waiters staring at you?'

Luke turned around and sure enough, the maitre'd and two waiters were looking in his direction.

'I've never brought anyone here with me before. I think they are all in shock.'

Luke laughed and felt as if he could now walk through the door Sadie had just opened for him, properly into her life.

'So what's worth thirty million pounds?'

'Well, it's a little technical, but you know how you pay with a contactless card?'

'You developed that?' Luke asked, incredulously.

'No, no. That is a radio frequency system. But any

merchant bank needs to be able to process the transaction and
that needs a particular piece of code. My company developed
this sort of crucial line of code and then trademarked it.'

'You sold a line of code for thirty million pounds?'

'Basically.'

Luke began to laugh, and laughed so hard that the
drinkers at other tables began to look over at them.

'That,' Luke said, 'is the most ridiculous thing I have ever
heard in my entire life.'

FIFTEEN

Rowdy had found nothing on any of the CCTV cameras stationed on the street where the yoga studio was located. She had even checked the cameras on streets several blocks over in all directions, but there was no sign of Chloe Little.

Hana was disappointed. She was convinced that Chloe Little had been looking for Luke.

'Are you sure?' Rowdy asked. 'There are other ways to get in contact with him. Even though he wasn't working here at the Met, if this was a police matter, why wouldn't she come directly to us? Even to pass on a message?'

'Yes, exactly. Something doesn't add up.'

'I know you asked me to get the CCTV footage from The Robson Hotel lobby bar, but I'm afraid that The Robson is refusing to send it over. Guest privacy, apparently. But they're not making a fuss about you looking at it. You'll have to go over there. I've told the manager that you'd be coming. You're not going to tell me why you want to see it?'

'Don't you like a surprise, Rowdy?'

Hana thanked her and began to make her way through

central London to The Robson. If Chloe Little was following Luke, she would be on this video footage. When she pulled up at the hotel entrance, the valet rushed out to park her car.

'I don't think I'm going to be that long. But feel free to move it,' Hana said as she tossed over her keys.

The manager was expecting her, as Rowdy said, and led Hana through a warren of small hallways one floor below the lobby level to the security office at the back of the hotel. Two men in black suits were sitting behind desks, each desk holding a large computer monitor. The room was sparse except for a couple of landline phones and a dozen filing cabinets lined up against one wall.

Hana must have looked surprised.

'Were you expecting a wall of twenty five little screens showing camera feeds?'

'Yeah, something like that,' Hana said.

'It's not Oceans Eleven. We don't have a casino vault in here. Much more discrete.'

Hana nodded. 'Sure. Where exactly do you have cameras in the hotel?'

'Not everywhere. We have the kind of clientele that expects complete discretion and privacy. So, most public areas, the entrance, elevator, the loading bay. No cameras in hallways or in staff areas. That breaks employment laws.'

'Okay, and Thursday evening?'

'Any particular area of the hotel, detective?'

'Why don't we start with the lobby bar, from six o'clock moving forward.'

The security manager input some information into the computer and up popped a split screen of the lobby bar, each side showing one half of the room. It was already bustling at six o'clock, the pre-dinner drinkers spanned across most of the available tables in the bar. Chloe Little was not among them.

The video was forwarded in fifteen minute intervals,

patrons coming and going. At the seven thirty mark, the video began to play again. Hana scanned both screens and then stopped breathing.

'There. Right there. She jabbed the screen with her finger. Can you rewind please?'

The video scrolled back in a blur, the figures on the screen rushing in static like a snowstorm.

'Play it from here.'

And there she was, at 7:21pm, waiting at the front of the bar to be seated. Hana watched as the maitre'd led her to a table for two in the centre of the bar and took off her coat, folding it over his arm before pulling out a chair and seating her.

Chloe looked around the bar, scanning each table and each guest. She looked behind her and did the same again. Then she tucked a strand of hair behind her ear and pulled her mobile phone out of the small purse she had placed on the table.

Hana didn't need to watch the rest of the video.

'Keep this up, don't touch it. I'm sending officers over to go through it.'

Jesus Christ, Hana thought as she rushed out of the room and forced her way past staff now crowding the hallway that led back up to the lobby and to the street. She grabbed her phone out of her pocket - no reception down here - and then she began to run towards the exit. She had to get reception. She had to call Luke. She felt slightly sick because as much as she liked to be proven right, this time she wished she wasn't.

Apart from Hana and Luke's therapist, there was only one other person on the planet who knew that Luke would normally have been sitting in that bar on a Thursday night.

SIXTEEN

FIFTEEN MONTHS EARLIER

Luke knew that Sadie would have gone to bed hours earlier and wouldn't be alarmed that he wasn't there in the house when she woke up in the morning. He and Hana had returned to the station just after one o'clock in the morning after interviewing Maggie Joseph. Apart from revealing that Marcus Wright had an office in Glasgow, she didn't have any other information about his work schedule or travel plans. They had no idea where Marcus Wright was and this meant one of two things. Either he had conveniently vanished on purpose or he had no idea that his life was about to be ripped apart.

Luke knew to be open-minded, which was his usual personality anyway, and if it was the latter situation, Marcus Wright needed to be found and told as soon as possible. So Luke sent Hana home and settled down at his desk, taking the opportunity to catch up on tedious paperwork. Every thirty minutes, he picked up the phone in front of him and punched in the numbers for Marcus Wright's mobile phone. Every single time the call didn't connect and went straight to voice mail. No messages were left.

It felt like a long night and Luke looked at the clock approaching seven and sent Sadie a text to let her know that he'd be home for a late breakfast, as soon as Hana returned to the office.

At seven thirty, he dialled the number again. It connected.

'Hello?'

Luke was so surprised that someone had answered, he bolted into a standing position. All alert bells rang in his head.

'Is this Marcus Wright?'

'Yes,' the voice said.

'Mr. Wright, this is Detective Chief Inspector Luke Wiley with the Metropolitan Police. Good morning. We have been trying to reach you overnight.'

There was a pause.

'I'm sorry. What is this about? Is everything alright?'

Luke hated that question, every single time.

'Where are you right now, Mr. Wright?'

'Glasgow train station. I just got off the Caledonian Sleeper train from London.'

Luke's tired brain spun a bit more quickly as he thought about his options. He snapped his fingers towards Hana who had just walked in the door with a coffee and a hot, buttered bagel in her hand. Hana knew to put down her breakfast and walked over to Luke.

Luke scribbled OFFICERS AT GLASGOW STATION NOW. INFO STAND. HAVE HIM onto a scrap of paper and shoved it at Hana. Hana nodded and pulled out her phone.

'Mr Wright. Are you still inside the station?'

'Yes.'

'Would you be so kind as to go immediately to the information stand in the ticket hall. It will be right in front of you somewhere. Officers will be there to meet you.'

There was another pause on the other end of the line.

'I'm sorry. What is going on here?'

Luke was the one to now take a pause. He considered his options again. How quickly would the officers be with Wright, was he actually in Glasgow train station, was this a diversion tactic? He decided to give Marcus Wright the benefit of the doubt.

'Mr. Wright. Do you see the information stand?'

'Yes, it's right in front of me. Do you see police officers?'

'No, there is no one here.'

Shit, Luke thought. Be faster Hana. Come on.

'Someone will be with you any moment now. I'm sorry to trouble you, and first thing in the morning, but we need some information from you and we prefer to speak to you in person. I'm sure that an officer will be with you any second now.'

'What on earth is this about?' Marcus Wright was beginning to become agitated and this wasn't ideal. Luke needed to keep him calm and more importantly, keep him inside that train station before he was lost to the streets of bustling Glasgow city. Luke could push police protocol, but he couldn't break it and he certainly couldn't lie to the man. He couldn't say that this was a routine call and that there was nothing to be concerned about.

'Again, I'm very sorry Mr. Wright. There is police business that needs some urgent attention and we believe you can assist us with this matter, so the officers in the station will be with you as quickly as they can so you can continue on with your day.'

Luke winced as soon as the words came out of his mouth —whatever his involvement, or not, Marcus Wright's day would not be continuing on as planned.

'Can this be quick please? I've just stepped off the

overnight train and have a very full day ahead of me. I'd like to be able to freshen up first and I don't have a lot of time. I'm standing here at the information stand and will wait just a couple of more minutes but then I'm afraid this will have to happen later.'

'Thank you, Mr. Wright. I really appreciate this. Would you just stay on the line with me please, until the officers arrive?'

Again, another pause.

'I'm sorry, can you tell me what this is about please?'

Hana, still standing across from Luke, now put down her phone and silently mouthed to him, 'On their way.'

Luke took a breath and waited for what he was about to do next. It was nudging firmly against protocol, but his assessment of the situation warranted it, or so he would tell O'Donnell later. Luke heard muffled sounds on the phone, as if it had been dropped to the side and brushing against a coat. He strained to hear what was happening, knowing that Marcus Wright was speaking with the officers who had finally reached him.

'Hello?' Marcus Wright said.

'Mr. Wright, the officers have reached you?'

'Yes.'

'Mr. Wright, I have to relay some upsetting news. The officers are there to assist you.'

Luke waited a beat, but there was no reply.

'I'm very sorry to inform you that your wife, Venetia, has died. I am so sorry. The officers are aware of the situation and will help you get back to London.'

'I'm sorry, I, I...don't understand.'

When the call ended a couple of minutes later and Luke had placed the phone handset down, he saw not just Hana but several other colleagues standing in the hallway staring at him, not waiting for him to say anything but just to support the gravity of the call in the room.

'I need Rowdy,' he said. 'Where is she?'

'I'll get her,' Hana replied. 'What do you need?'

'The train times of the Caledonian Sleeper and the CCTV from Glasgow station pulled up. Right now.'

─────

Venetia Wright hadn't left the cocktail bar until ten past ten. The Caledonian Sleeper pulled out of Euston Station at exactly 9:32pm. Rowdy had checked the exact engineering timesheet for the night — there had been no delays.

The CCTV was pulled up and ready to view on the screen in the incident room. Luke and Hana sat down and prepared to watch it.

'There's only one camera feed that Rowdy pulled up here. The platform that the sleeper pulls into is the furthest east in the station and there aren't ticket barriers to exit through there. No need apparently, as all tickets are checked on the train on that service.'

'So we're looking at just the main hall?'

'Yes, where the information stand is located. It should be all there. Luke, it does look like he was on that train.'

Hana had spoken to the detective who had joined the officers at Glasgow station. They had been able to move quickly. Marcus Wright was taken directly to the station for eventual transport back to London and the train was sealed off as soon as passengers had all disembarked.

Marcus Wright had occupied a Club room, the nicest on the service with a large double bed and ensuite bathroom, complete with a personal shower. The bed had been slept in. The train manager had confirmed that Wright had boarded early, just after

8pm when the club carriages opened to serve dinner and drinks in their dining car. This was popular with business travellers who had a bite to eat and then settled into their rooms before the train departed London, hoping to get a good night's sleep.

The barman was interviewed and said that Wright had been quite chatty, ordering a glass of white wine and a burrata salad and sat in the dining car until around 9pm. He declined to have breakfast served in his room, said good night to the manager and went to bed.

'Let's see it,' Luke said and Hana pressed 'play' on the monitor.

Glasgow Station was particularly quiet at 7:30am on a Saturday morning. Luke and Hana watched the stream of passengers entering the ticket hall having just stepped off the Caledonian Sleeper, pulling small cases behind them, slightly bleary-eyed. No one was moving very quickly and it was easy to spot Marcus Wright walking down the centre of the hall. He was wearing a Barbour jacket and carrying a small duffel bag in his left hand. He stopped walking suddenly, and stuck his hand into his right coat pocket, fishing around for something. He pulled out his phone and stared at the screen. For a full ten seconds he stood on the spot looking at his phone, then he raised it to his ear.

'Did he take that long to pick up?' Hana asked.

Luke shook his head.

They continued to watch Marcus Wright, observers from the other side of an event they had already lived through. They were both waiting for the moment that the officers appeared. There it was, Wright's hand still holding the phone but dropping it towards his chest, the mouthpiece muffled by zipper of his coat.

He placed the phone back up to his ear.

He was very still.

He leaned forward slightly.

Then Marcus Wright bent over and the phone dropped out of his hand. One officer rushed forward to grab Wright before he fell. The other stood by quietly and then stooped down to pick up the phone. They were told that shortly afterwards, once they had taken Marcus Wright outside, he had been sick.

Hana pressed pause. 'What do you think? A good actor?'

Luke shook his head one more time before offering his verdict.

'Or a completely broken man.'

SEVENTEEN

The overwhelming emotion that Michael felt as soon as Detectives Hackett and Smith had left his house at mid-day on Saturday, having informed him that Chloe Little was dead, was relief.

He was relieved at this stroke of exceptionally lucky timing that Lottie and both boys were not home, having gone out to pick up supplies for an upcoming school camping trip. The detectives hadn't stayed long, having asked him where he had been the night before and if Chloe had called him at anytime during the previous few days.

He told one truth and one lie, which he figured was safe enough. Any discrepancies in what he had said could believably be explained by a busy life and not remembering exact timings.

Michael had also felt rising irritation as the detectives questioned his role with Venetia's committee. Why was this relevant? Shouldn't they have been looking for who had killed Chloe last night? What on earth had Lucy and Nigel said to them?

Michael wasn't the sort of person to dwell on what

couldn't be changed. But he sure as hell wasn't going to be dragged into something that was going to affect the rest of his life. He would have to speak to Lucy and Nigel and figure out what they knew — and what they had said.

He looked at the clock on the wall in his kitchen and figured that Lottie and the boys wouldn't be back for another half an hour or so. Michael picked up his phone and slipped out the back door and walked across the small garden towards his office. He fumbled in the planter sitting next to the shed door and found the key, letting himself inside.

Sitting down at his desk, he debated on who to phone to set up a meeting. Phone Nigel and listen to him ramble on incessantly about the police and Chloe and their situations and not be able to get a word in. No, he wanted to hear all of this when Lucy was in the room as well. It was possible that he was going to need some support with any next steps that needed to be taken.

So he unlocked his phone and pulled up the missed calls screen, took a breath, and pressed Lucy's name.

'Hi, Michael.'

Lucy sounded dreadful, like she had been in bed for a week with the flu.

'Are you alright?' he asked. 'Are you feeling okay?'

'Chloe is dead, Michael. How do you think I am feeling?' She began to cry, which clearly had been what she had been doing when he called.

'I know,' Michael said. 'It's just dreadful. I think I'm in shock.'

Lucy didn't say anything, taking a moment to wonder if this was actually the case.

'Look, Lucy. I think we all need to talk. You, me and Nigel. We need to get our story straight.'

'What story, Michael.' Lucy did not pose this as a question.

'You know that she phoned me last night?' Lucy continued. 'She was hysterical about what you had done to her.'

'I didn't know she had called you,' Michael said, very quietly.

'What do you want me to say here? That all is forgiven? I'll meet with you, and I'll call Nigel to meet as well, but then I want nothing else to do with either of you. I'm out.'

'Really? I'm kind of surprised to hear that.'

'Chloe was maybe doing the right thing, Michael.'

————

Lucy refused to let Michael come to her flat. The last thing she wanted was those two men alone with her. Who could she trust at this point? Michael seemed angry when she insisted on meeting in a public space, but they agreed to meet at the Caffè Nero close to South Kensington station the next day at noon. She said that she would call Nigel and tell him to be there as well.

'But what if he can't make that time?' Michael said.

'Jesus Michael, what the hell else is he going to be doing?'

————

After Michael had hung up, he sat alone in his office and felt a wave of tiredness wash over him. He opened the bottom drawer of the filing cabinet that was nestled beneath his desk and pulled out the file folder from the very back of the unit.

Flipping through its contents, he found what he was looking for and stopped short, his breath catching in his chest.

The photograph wasn't of great quality. Chloe said that she had plugged her phone into a kiosk at the pharmacy when she saw the machine that printed photos instantly. She said she'd done it on a whim because it had been such a wonderful picture of them. She printed one for herself and one for him.

Michael had felt a rush of different emotions when Chloe handed it to him. He felt tickled that she had done this for him, but also anxious that something so physical was now in his possession. Staring at the photograph now, he had to admit that it was an incredible photograph of them both. Captured mid-laughter, Chloe's head thrown back with her long brunette hair streaming perfectly off her face, Michael leaning towards her grinning, his hand on her thigh.

EIGHTEEN

Hana, for once, didn't quite know what to do. She stopped short coming out of The Robson, noting that her car was still parked on the street where she had left it. The valet nodded to her as if he'd done her a favour.

She smiled a thank you and walked to the car, opened the door and sat down. She held the ignition key in her hand as she tried to figure out what to do. Should she drive to Luke's house to tell him, or call him right away from where she was?

Hana was never indecisive, but she had to tell Luke what she had just seen on the CCTV and what this meant and she knew that it would upset him. She really didn't want to upset him.

How was this happening? This old case with its open wounds was suddenly in front of them again. It felt like a giant hazard on the road — no way around it until they dealt with it. Hana decided that she would drive over to Luke's and speak to him about what she had seen in person but as she pulled out into traffic she realized that she was merely choosing to put off what she knew she had to do. She shook her head and sighed to herself. She also knew that she couldn't bring herself to walk up those steps to Luke's front door and enter it with this kind of news. The moment she had made the same trip just over a year earlier had been probably the worst moment of her life.

Hana connected to the bluetooth and dialled Luke's number.

'How did you get on?' Luke said, picking up immediately.

'Uh, good. I mean, nothing on the CCTV around the yoga studio. But we did pick something else up,' Hana said.

'And?'

'Luke, I was right. Chloe Little was definitely looking for you. She was in the lobby bar at The Robson on Thursday night. CCTV has it.'

'You've seen the video?'

'Yes. I've just left The Robson. They wouldn't release the CCTV but officers are going over there now to scan all of the tape. She got to the hotel around a little before 7:30pm and sat at a table right in the centre of the bar. She was alone.'

There was silence on the other end of the phone.

'I didn't watch the entire tape. We'll get it sent over to Rowdy now that it is formally connected to a crime. But I, well, I obviously needed to speak to you right away.'

'Hana, you know what this means.'

Hana did know what it meant.

'Yes. I'm sorry. I don't know what to say.'

'Only three people would know that I go to The Robson on Thursday nights. Well, four people, but one of them is dead.'

'I know, Luke.'

Luke's voice didn't become raised, as Hana suspected it might. He didn't seem distressed by what he said next. He just sounded like he was living inside a life he no longer recognized and he sounded quiet, but an angry kind of quiet.

'You would know I would be in The Robson. Nicky Bowman would know I would be in The Robson.'

Hana completed the trifecta for him.

'And Marcus Wright.'

'Yes,' Luke said. 'And Marcus Wright.'

―――――

FIFTEEN MONTHS EARLIER

When Marcus Wright had been picked up by officers in Glasgow Station after Luke had relayed the devastating news about his wife, all parties concerned figured that the quickest way to get Marcus back to London was to fly him down.

Luke drove to Heathrow alone that day while Hana stayed behind in the station to pull more pieces of Venetia Wright's life together. It had been a brutal crime in a relatively busy part of central London and without any clear cut evidence or a prime suspect, they had to work quickly to map out the daily life of a busy, and as far as they could determine, well-liked woman.

Luke hadn't been entirely sure what to expect as he drove down the M4 towards the airport. What can you know about a person from a brief phone call? Not a lot. Marcus had been polite, but irritated by the intrusion. Fair enough. The Scottish officers who assisted Marcus in Glasgow reported that he had been in shock and understandably frantic. They needed information from Marcus - and a lot of it - as quickly and efficiently as possible before the killer could slip away from them. Often in these cases where the victim's next of kin held the clues they needed but was struggling to function in such difficult circumstances, getting the family member as comfortable as possible was the best way forward. Luke needed to establish a good rapport with Marcus and get him talking as clearly and thoughtfully as possible and he had made the call with O'Donnell already that this would be done in the familiar and comfortable surroundings of the home of Marcus and Venetia Wright. Luke would drive Marcus home, and Hana and forensic officers would be waiting for them there. They had not yet entered the Wright residence and needed to get in that house searching for anything to help them right away.

Dark ash coloured clouds filled the sky above Luke and he switched on his headlights. The heat of the last few days was about to break with a thunderstorm and Luke was happy he wasn't on that plane with Marcus Wright. It was going to be a bumpy descent. As he pulled off the motorway onto the slip road full of taxis and Ubers, splatters of rain began to hit the windshield. By the time Luke had pulled up at arrivals and showed his credentials to the security staff, the heavens had truly opened and rain lashed down onto the pavement, pooling on the concrete as there was too much water to properly drain off. Luke didn't even bother to jump the puddles as he made his way through the automatic doors and into the bustling arrivals hall. With no checked luggage and no immigration hall to navigate, Marcus Wright and the accompanying Scottish officer appeared quickly at the barrier separating arriving passengers and their loved ones awaiting them. Luke had been watching the eager faces of those waiting, some with flowers, some with bouncing children in tow. He was acutely aware of the reason he was waiting for Marcus Wright and that it was not Venetia waiting at the barrier for her husband. There was never going to be a happy reunion for Marcus.

'Mr. Wright,' Luke said, stepping forward to the pair of men. 'I'm Detective Chief Inspector Luke Wiley. I was the person who called you when you arrived in Glasgow this morning.'

Marcus Wright looked at Luke and nodded.

'I am deeply sorry for your loss, Mr. Wright. Let's get you

out of here and home right away. If you'll follow me, please.'

Luke finished the sign off with the accompanying officer and led Marcus outside to his car, both of them getting drenched as Luke opened the front passenger door and gestured for Marcus get in.

Marcus Wright wasn't someone you would instantly recognize if you'd previously met him. Bumping into him on the street, you would take a moment to remember where you'd seen him before and under what circumstances your paths had crossed. He wasn't someone who would stand out in a crowd. Marcus was of average build, sandy brown hair, and Luke wasn't surprised to see that the man sitting next to him matched the voice he heard on the phone. He could more clearly see what he was wearing that had been only patches of blurry colour on the CCTV footage. Brown loafers, jeans, a checked collared shirt, and dark green Barbour jacket. He looked like the sort of person you'd approach on the street to ask for directions. This average looking man stared ahead at the congested traffic in front of them, the most extreme circumstance thrust upon him.

'Are you alright, Marcus? There is a bottle of water next to you,' Luke gestured to the cup holder between them. 'I hope it's alright if I call you Marcus.'

'Yes, of course. That's fine.'

They sat in silence for a couple of minutes as Luke maneuvered through the tunnels around Heathrow, eventually merging back onto the motorway towards the city. Luke would remember later how this felt like a comfortable silence.

'I'm sorry,' Marcus offered. 'I just can't believe this is happening.'

'I understand. We will get you home and brief you as quickly as we can. There will be supporting officers to assist you as well.'

Marcus was so still next to him in the passenger seat that it was only when Luke heard a series of quick, sharp, audible intakes of breath did he realize that Marcus was crying.

'Would you like me to use the lights and sirens to get you home more quickly? I can do that - it's just not the most comfortable ride.'

'No, it's okay,' Marcus said. 'I'm fine.'

'I'll go as quickly as I can.'

'Thank you,' Marcus said quietly. 'The officers in Glasgow said that she had been stabbed. Is that right?'

'Yes, I'm afraid so.'

Marcus shook his head.

'I just don't understand. Venetia doesn't deserve this. She is a wonderful person. Just the best person. Why wasn't Maggie with her? I wanted to call her but the officers have asked that I speak to you first.'

'Yes,' said Luke. 'My partner and I have already spoken to Maggie and her husband. I'm sorry but we need to brief you. It's the best way to get whoever did this and we need to do this as quickly as possible.'

The rest of the journey into London was quiet, Marcus looking out the window and Luke focusing on the road in front of him. Only when they approached the exit that would take them down into Holland Park, the west London neighbourhood where the Wrights lived, did Marcus speak again.

'Ignore the GPS,' he said, just as Luke was glancing at the screen to the right of the steering wheel. It's faster to continue on and turn left down Ladbroke Grove.'

'Okay, thanks.'

As they pulled up to the house, a large Victorian detached building, the driveway behind an electronic gate.

'I'm sorry,' Marcus said. 'I don't have the clicker for the gate. Venetia always holds onto it.' He began to cry again and seemed to crumple into his seat.

'It's not a problem,' Luke said, looking at the armada of

police cars on the street. Forensics, Hana, uniformed police, victim support officers — neighbours looking through their curtains would think that Venetia Wright was murdered right here.

After explaining the procedure of what was about to happen, who was to go where in the house, and obtaining Marcus's permission to do so, Luke and Hana walked Marcus to the front door, watched him unlock it and step inside. The house alarm was sounding and he moved down the hall to open the small panel on the wall and turn it off.

'Did Venetia always turn the alarm on before leaving the house?' Hana asked.

'Yes,' Marcus replied. 'But we left the house together last night. I...I don't remember who turned it on.'

'Oh, that's okay,' Hana said, suddenly very aware of this man's fragile state. Marcus looked towards Luke, his eyes pleading, as if the answer to who had set the alarm would tell them exactly who had killed his wife.

'Why don't you show us where you would like to sit down and have a chat with us, Marcus.' Luke smiled at him, hoping to sound encouraging, when both he and Hana knew that there were many difficult questions ahead over the next hour.

Marcus led them down the hall towards the back of the large house. Every room they passed seemed enormous due to the tall ceilings — they had to be at least twelve feet high. Luke and Hana followed him into a spacious living room that was framed on one side by enormous French doors that led out into the back garden. The room was so large, it had two distinct seating areas, one on the opposite side from the windows with leather armchairs and foot hassocks, a slightly worn Persian rug that ran down the length of the room towards a towering wall of bookshelves. It was designed as a reading nook and Luke imagined Venetia sitting there, feet stretched out in front of her with a glass of wine and a good book. He always tried to imagine the victim in the most comfortable part of their daily life — it was often this space where crucial clues revealed themselves.

The other seating area consisted of two large sofas that faced each other, easily seating four people each. The centre-piece of the room that invited the sofas to take up this space was a fireplace, its mantel holding a clock and three china vases, all with small leopard heads in different poses coming out of the them. The focal point of the fireplace was its surround — in the place of pillars on each side of the grate were two tall, grey elephants. They were carved out of marble, ears fanning out to the side, the trunks turned in towards the centre of the fireplace from each side, tusks jutting out ever so slightly. The elephants were phenomenal and unusual to be in a house, the kind of ornamental design you'd maybe see in the entranceway of a grand colonial hotel in the Far East.

Marcus sat down on one of the sofas and shrugged off his coat, leaving it sitting in a lump behind him. Hana and Luke took a place opposite him.

'I understand how difficult all of this is for you, Marcus,' Luke began.

Marcus suddenly stood up and moved towards the book-shelves to the right of the fireplace. They ran floor to ceiling and Marcus moved the bookshelf ladder along its rail slightly, reaching into the bookshelf.

The fireplace leapt to life.

'I'm sorry, I know it's quite warm outside, but I don't like sitting in this room without the fireplace on. It's always slightly chilly in here. I never understood at first why Venetia had this converted to a gas fireplace — I hated it at first — but now I love it. I can turn it off if you'd like?'

Hana realized that this man was still in a state of shock. Marcus was aware of what was happening but needed the distraction to make the situation tolerable. She felt sorry for him but she needed him to provide some much needed answers.

'Mr. Wright,' Hana said, 'that's just fine. It is a bit chilly in here with this rain. It's quite something, the fireplace. I'm not sure I've ever seen one like it.'

'Oh yes,' Marcus said, looking up at Hana gratefully, as though he was able to talk about this without hesitation or anguish.

'The elephants are certainly unusual,' Hana remarked.

'Aren't they? Venetia saw them in India — she loves India. She had them shipped back to London and then found a stonemason to properly install them here.'

'Are the leopard vases from India as well?'

'No. Actually those are from Sri Lanka. There used to be four of them, but one just broke sadly.'

Luke sat up a bit straighter.

'How did that happen?' he said.

'The cleaner,' Luke replied. 'Accident, unfortunately.'

'You and your wife have certainly done quite a bit of travel,' Hana said.

'Yes, a bit. I mean...these trips here,' Marcus pointed towards the objects on the fireplace, 'Venetia did these trips before we met. But I have been to India, it is a very special place to her and she wanted to show me...'

At this mention of his wife and this memory that must be flashing through his mind, Marcus began to break down again.

'I'm sorry,' Marcus said. 'I just don't understand what is happening.'

Luke nodded at him. 'Shall we start now, Marcus? Let's talk about yesterday.'

Luke and Hana spent the next half hour pulling the events of the previous day out of Marcus. Nothing was out of the ordinary. He had gone to his office in Chancery Lane. Venetia had spent the day at home answering emails and doing laundry. When he got home around 5pm, Venetia was eating a bowl of pasta that she had whipped up so she could have dinner before heading out to meet Maggie for a drink or two. Marcus and Venetia had spoken on the phone earlier in the day and he had said he would board his train to Glasgow early and eat in the club dining car before it departed, so she only made enough pasta for one.

Marcus had packed a change of clothes and they left the house together by taxi for Euston Station around a quarter past seven. The taxi had stopped on the Euston Road a few blocks shy of the station where Venetia had hopped out and headed south into Fitzrovia to the cocktail bar.

'Did you speak to your wife again before the train left?' Luke asked.

'No. She didn't have her phone. She hardly ever takes it out with her. I had just pulled my phone out at Glasgow station to call her when you called me.'

The two detectives now had the details of the last twelve hours of Venetia Wright's life and everything looked like it added up. Did something happen in the hours that Venetia was alone at home? Something that Marcus wouldn't know?

'Marcus,' Luke said. 'You're not aware of anyone who may have wished harm to your wife? An employee or an ex-partner?'

Marcus shook his head. 'I really don't think so. Do you think this was targeted? I just can't imagine that. Everyone loved Venetia. She's an only child, was single forever before we met, and she doesn't employ anyone. I mean, she works with a dozen or so different charities and there are people involved with her there, but they are mostly volunteers, I think.'

'How long have you two been together?'

'We just had our five year anniversary,' Marcus said, looking towards the fireplace and trying to control his breath, which had begun to stutter into tears again.

'And how did you meet?' Asked Hana.

'Like everyone else these days, I guess. Online. We were so lucky.'

As Marcus tried to pull himself together, the lead forensic officer appeared at the entrance to the living room and Luke stood up to speak to him. Their team had finished their initial look through the house, collecting Venetia's laptop and phone for further examination at the station and had been careful not to disturb anything else. Only the two victim support officers remained in the house, waiting to speak to Marcus Wright and offer whatever they could to help the grieving man sitting in front of them.

With assurances that they would be in touch with Marcus first thing tomorrow, or earlier if there was news to relay, Luke and Hana said their goodbyes and began the hand off to the waiting officers.

'I'm sorry,' Marcus said. 'But Detective Wiley? Would you please stay?'

Hana looked at Luke, wondering what he was going to do.

'I'd be very happy to stay with the support officers for a bit, Marcus. That's no problem.'

'No,' Marcus said. 'I'm sure they are very good but I think I'm fine. I don't need that sort of assistance. I...I just would prefer to not be alone at the moment. Would you stay?'

This was unusual and later Luke would look back at this moment wishing that he had left the officers to it and had left with Hana, walking out of Marcus Wright's front door and back to the station.

Instead, Luke had nodded to the officers and to Hana and watched them leave without him.

Marcus and Luke were left alone in the house, the rain still pelting the windows. Marcus had offered Luke a glass of wine, which he declined. And then Marcus poured himself a large glass of red, sat back down on the sofa and began to talk.

NINETEEN

Caffè Nero at noon on a weekend was an absolute zoo. It was just how Lucy wanted it. She got there half an hour early, ordered a latte and then waited out a family of four who had the prize table in the corner, slightly away from everyone else. She swooped for it as they stood up to leave and then spent the next thirty minutes guarding it from tourists, students and exasperated mothers.

Nigel, predictably, was right on time and leaned in to hug her. She accepted the embrace awkwardly, realizing that he must be terribly upset that Chloe was dead. He offered to get her another coffee and she thanked him, her eyes scanning the cafe entrance for Michael.

Lucy watched Nigel in the queue for the barista. Could she trust him? He was the odd one out of their little group — slightly awkward, but always well meaning. She had always assumed that he was around Michael's age, but seemed older. He was the only one of the four of them that didn't have a prior connection before joining Venetia's committee. Chloe and Lucy had met Venetia in India and she had been a whirlwind of energy. They had accompanied her to one of the schools she helped fund through her charity and the children had adored her. Then it had been back to their little hotel on the beach for beer and good curry and so much laughter. It wasn't hard for both women to volunteer for the charity when they returned to London. Venetia had said it was fate that they all met on that day in this little village on the Goan coast.

'An elementary school teacher and a lawyer. It's too perfect!' Venetia had said. And she had been right — Lucy found herself developing bits of the curriculum for parts of the school program and Chloe worked several extra hours each week, after her already long working day, to negotiate the legal red tape of an overseas charity. But Venetia was the kind of person you wanted to do things for, that you wanted to work with, and so you put in the hours. Lucy took an involuntary deep breath just thinking about Venetia and how they had felt about her, and how everything had turned out.

Nigel was still waiting to collect their coffees and was chatting to the person waiting next to him. Always involving himself in other peoples' lives, always wanting to be included. He was incredibly annoying, but Lucy also felt sorry for him. She knew there wasn't much going on in his life. He had been the one to see an advertisement for volunteer work with one of their charity drives — she can't even remember which one — and had somehow infiltrated their committee. He had taken to Chloe immediately and you couldn't blame him. Did she feel a bit put out that it wasn't her that Nigel took a shine to? Maybe briefly, but she was also happy to not be on the receiving end of his attention and of the two women, Chloe was always going to be the one that men were attracted to first. She had gotten used to that.

Just as Nigel was predictably early for their coffee meeting, Michael was predictably late. It had been Lucy's invitation that brought Michael to their committee. The previous school year Lucy had taught Michael's youngest son and had gotten to know both Michael and his wife throughout the year. It was Lottie that she initially knew better as she did most of the school runs and when Lucy had mentioned that they were looking for someone with a financial background to help with the fiscal and budgetary side of the charity, Lottie immediately offered her husband's services. Little did she know how much she could come to regret that. And that was the thing — Lottie still did not know the half of it. Now Chloe was dead, the remaining three committee members were in a catastrophic mess and she didn't know who she could trust.

Michael finally walked in the door, spotted Lucy and half-heartedly waved as he began to squeeze his way past other customers towards her. She suddenly felt relieved that Nigel was there too.

The two men got to the table at the same time, Michael shaking off Nigel's offer to go back and get him a coffee as well.

'No, I'm fine. I'm not exactly feeling like a coffee or anything to eat.'

The three of them sat for a moment in silence, not knowing what to say, how to begin. They all were acutely aware of the empty fourth chair sitting next to them.

'Did the police come to you both as well?' Michael asked. 'Do we know what happened? I just can't believe it.'

'It's just terrible,' Nigel said. 'Chloe was killed. She was actually *murdered*,' he whispered.

'I'm sure we are all in shock,' Michael said.

'Are we?' Lucy piped up. 'It's a terrible shock to me that Chloe is dead. How much of a shock is it to you, Michael?'

Michael's mouth dropped open. He looked as though he truly could not believe what he was hearing. Like he had been punched.

'Are you serious, Lucy? What the hell?'

Nigel looked dumbfounded and Lucy noticed.

'What, Nigel. You didn't also think this?'

'I don't know what to think, Lucy. I've been thinking about Chloe. She has been *killed*,' he whispered again. 'It's just terrible. We don't know what happened. The police said she was on her way home.'

'On her way home from where, exactly?' Lucy whipped around to look at Michael as she spoke.

'Are you serious?' Michael asked. 'I'm sorry, Lucy. I can't believe the accusation you are throwing out here. And keep your voice down.'

Anger rose in Lucy like a tidal wave and she could almost hear the blood rushing into her ears.

'This does affect all of us equally, Lucy,' Michael spat back.

'Really,' she said. 'Well, only one of us was fucking her.'

Lucy wasn't sure who looked more wounded by her words — Michael or Nigel. Both men looked incredibly uncomfortable.

Michael leaned in and looked carefully at Nigel and Lucy as the noise of the cafe patrons clattered around them. He wanted them to hear him clearly with what he was about to say.

'Can I please remind you both that we are all still in the same situation here?' Michael lowered his voice and spoke softly. 'I'm afraid that Chloe's death doesn't change that.'

'Yes, I agree with Michael,' Nigel said, swallowing hard.

Michael nodded and continued. 'What did Chloe say when she called you both?'

'Well, what did she say to *you*, Michael?' Lucy snapped back.

'I didn't speak to her yesterday,' Michael bit his lip. 'We weren't really speaking.'

'And you expect us to believe that?'

'Ask the police if you don't believe me, Lucy. That's the reason they *did* come to speak to me. The detectives said that Chloe made three calls just before she was killed. One they couldn't trace and the other two were to you both. They wanted to know why I thought Chloe had called you two and why she didn't call me if the only reason we know each other is through the committee. So you can probably see why I'm a little bit nervous here.'

'You think that Chloe told the police about what happened before she was killed?' Nigel ventured.

Michael shrugged and sat back in his chair.

Nigel realized that he had to tell them.

'Well,' he said, 'Chloe did say on the call to me that she was going to talk to the detective that led Venetia's murder case.'

'Detective Wiley?' Michael asked.

'Yes.'

'She had mentioned this to me a little while ago. I thought I had talked her out of it. Everything seemed fine, everything had been just fine and I didn't understand why she was feeling so anxious. It's not like any of this was our fault.'

'Are you serious?' Lucy said. 'All of this is our fault.'

There was silence around the table. Any of the other customers in Caffe Nero who happened to look over at this stony threesome in the corner table would have wondered what on earth they were discussing and probably relieved to not be a part of it. They all looked miserable.

'Look,' Michael said. 'There is absolutely no point in rehashing any of the past now. For better or for worse, we *are* all still in this situation and we have a really big problem if Chloe spoke to Detective Wiley. What did she say when she called you, Lucy?'

For the second time that weekend, Lucy told one truth and one lie.

'Basically the same. She was feeling upset and guilty about everything and wanted to sound out the detective from Venetia's murder case. She said he wasn't working for the police anymore and so she thought she could get some advice which maybe would help our situation.'

Michael and Nigel looked like they were going to be sick and Lucy sat back in her chair. Chloe had spoken to her with exactly these words — but that was a week ago. What she had told Lucy on the phone had been something entirely different.

TWENTY

Luke wanted to see the CCTV for himself. Hana was waiting for him outside the front entrance of Scotland Yard, a coffee in her hand.

'What are you doing out here?' Luke said, as he strode across the promenade leading from the Thames towards the building.

'Needed a bit of peace and quiet,' Hana shouted above the honking cars frustrated by gridlock traffic on the Embankment on a weekend afternoon.

'Besides,' she said, 'someone's got to escort you in.'

'Oh no,' Luke replied, reaching into the inner pocket of his worn, brown leather jacket and pulling out the familiar black card wallet emblazoned with the Metropolitan Police crest. He flashed it open at Hana, revealing a blemish-free, sparkling new ID card.

'Rowdy works quickly,' she said.

'Shall we?' Luke gestured towards the entrance.

'Oh god, I hope O'Donnell is in today,' Hana said as she took off the lid of her cup and dumped the rest of the milky liquid into the planter next to her. 'I would hate to miss the look on his face the first time you walk back in there.'

'You and I wish for different things, Hana.'

O'Donnell was, indeed in and hunched over a laptop next to Rowdy as Luke and Hana stepped off the elevator. The look on his face was that of thunder, while Rowdy beamed at them both.

'I'll be right with you, Wiley,' she said. This did not exactly improve O'Donnell's mood.

Luke nodded and winked at her before he and Hana moved down the corridor and into the office that used to belong to Detective Chief Inspector Luke Wiley. It was now empty, the name plate gone from the door, the photograph of Sadie no longer sitting on the desk. Missing were the other random assortment of objects that Luke used to have — a penguin pen holder that he'd been given in a secret Santa gift draw during his early days on the force that he had carried from desk to desk with him. A brass train key that had been his father's. A handful of smooth pebbles in various shapes and colours from different beaches, picking them up and slipping them into a pocket a habit he has had since he was a boy.

Hana knew he was thinking about this paraphernalia as Luke looked at the desk.

'Going to bring everything back?'

He reached over and squeezed her arm.

'Not quite yet.'

Hana hopped up into a seated position on the desk while Luke opened the filing cabinet on the wall, looking to see if anything was left in there. Like the rest of the office, it was empty.

'I'm surprised this space wasn't immediately taken over,' Luke said. 'Space is a premium in this building.'

'Oh, it was,' Hana said. 'There was a guy who moved right

in, quit a month later. Left the force entirely. Too much to live up to taking over your office.'

Luke rolled his eyes. They took a moment to look at each other and savour what they had both been missing for the past fifteen months. Luke at home alone, mired in grief and disbelief and anger at himself. Hana floating from partner to partner, steadfastly refusing any permanent assignment because she couldn't bear it. Finally, they were back together, seemingly where they belonged. But the moment didn't last long. They knew that something sinister was at play, there was a dead woman and no prime suspect, and they were running out of time.

'Why do you think Chloe Little was looking for you?'

'Well,' Luke said. 'To tell me something, clearly. And it has to be about Venetia Wright — that's the connection.'

'And to know you would be in The Robson on a Thursday night?'

Luke nodded. 'There's only one explanation. She *has* to have spoken to Marcus Wright.'

'I know what you are thinking Luke and it's a really, really bad idea.'

'Hana.'

'I'm serious. Hackett or Smith will go. Hell, I'll go.'

'Absolutely not.'

'Luke.'

'*Hana.*' Now Luke's voice was firm, and slightly raised. 'I will speak to Marcus Wright. End of discussion.'

A gentle knock on the glass window of the office interrupted their argument.

'May I?' Rowdy poked her head inside and without waiting for an answer walked in and set up her laptop on the desk.

The three of them looked at the CCTV footage from The

Robson. Chloe Little was already scanning the lobby bar while she was waiting to be seated.

'Look,' Hana said as she pointed to the maitre d' checking his tablet on the podium by the bar entrance, pressing the screen and then welcoming Chloe with a flourish of the arm.

'She had a reservation. She had planned this.'

But the rest of the footage revealed nothing of note. Chloe sipped one glass of wine, refused the food menu and occasionally looked at her phone. This went on for 45 minutes until she looked at her phone one final time and typed a message. They watched her wait for response, type something else and then immediately beckon a waiter for the bill.

'She was called away to something,' Hana said.

'Or was warned off,' Luke replied.

They watched as the bill was presented to her, Chloe tapped her card on the machine to pay, pocketed the receipt and left the way she came.

While he never usually thought about it, watching Chloe tap with her card to pay in this setting that he loved with his wife, made Luke wince slightly.

'Which way does she exit the hotel?' asked Hana.

'Same way she came in,' said Rowdy. 'Out the front door and then we have her making her way through Mayfair towards Park Lane. She gets on the 74 bus and gets off at South Ken station. Then, I'm afraid, it's Thursday night in South Ken. A little busy and we lose her. Officers are canvassing restaurants and bars and convenience stores around the station but nothing yet.'

They look at the time stamps and there is about an hour between Chloe stepping off the bus and the approximate time of death according to the coroner.

'There's a lot you can do in an hour,' said Hana.

'Or not. It takes only a few minutes to make three phone calls.'

Rowdy shut the laptop and asked the detectives if she could do anything else for them.

'Yeah, one thing,' said Hana. 'You could talk him out of speaking to Marcus Wright.'

Luke was expecting Rowdy to chime in and to have to calmly explain why he had to be the one to go and speak to Marcus face to face.

'A bit late for that, Hana,' Rowdy said. 'Hackett and Smith have already been to see Marcus Wright. They got nothing.'

'What do you mean?' asked Luke.

'He refused to speak to them. Told them that he would only speak to you.'

TWENTY-ONE

Michael did feel a bit queasy as he walked out of Caffè Nero. It wasn't a particularly productive talk and the three of them left agreeing to say nothing to the police if they were questioned again. Could Michael trust Lucy and Nigel? Before the meeting he thought he could, but he was terribly taken aback by everything Lucy had said. She had come this close to straight out accusing Michael of murdering Chloe.

Michael swallowed and tried to quell the uneasy feeling in his stomach. This situation did not need to unravel because frankly, the most dangerous element in the whole thing was dead. Chloe was the one who had slipped into her guilt while the others had been able to just get on with their lives. Or so he thought.

He had expected that Lucy and Nigel would have been more sympathetic. They knew he was having an affair with Chloe. If it hadn't been clear from Lucy's comments just now, he and Chloe already knew that the others had figured it out. Chloe had promised him that she hadn't told Lucy anything, but he knew she had been lying. It didn't bother him — he understood how good girl friends operated and Michael trusted that she would keep her mouth shut.

But Chloe was dead and Michael had kept his quiet devastation to himself. There were times he felt that they truly were meant to be together and he was going to leave Lottie, but in the end it just couldn't happen. He was not going to break up his family for a fling.

He thought back to that first time Chloe flirted with him. He had been surprised - and thrilled. She was gorgeous and her lingering hand on the small of his back as they said goodbye one night, the way she brushed something off the collar of his jacket afterwards and leaned in to kiss him on the cheek. It was incredibly sexy, as was Chloe, and he felt no hesitation in that moment in asking if she'd like to grab a quick glass of wine at a pub down the road from Venetia's house before heading home.

It had been an easy slide into an affair from there. Dinners out, a quick drink in the bar that was smack between their respective offices, only blocks from each other in the City. Four months in, there had been a glorious weekend when Lottie had taken the boys to see her parents and he had begged off, citing too much work. Chloe and Michael had holed up together in her house in Fulham, leaving only once to buy more wine and some chives that she wanted to add to her salad. He can picture her standing in her kitchen at the counter, wearing nothing but his button up shirt which only reached the very top of her thighs and kept slipping down over her shoulder to expose her collarbone. She snipped the chives into a large bowl and brought it to the table she had set for two. They had cooked and made love and talked all weekend, cocooned in her beautiful, quiet home. He had loved every minute of it, and that was probably why he had said the two things that changed the course of their lives.

The first thing he said was a mistake — he had been caught

up in the moment. They were comfortable, and they talked -
really talked - and she listened to him. She was encouraging,
and their time together felt ecstatic and the sex was incredible.
Michael told her that he was thinking about leaving his wife so
that they could be together. He hadn't felt immediately that
saying this had been a mistake. Chloe didn't react except to
smile and nod and take his head in her hands and place tiny
kisses on his temples, his nose, the crease between his
eyebrows.

The second thing he said was later that night in bed. They
lay still slightly entangled, sipping glasses of red wine when he
voiced the idea that had been brewing for a couple of months.
Something that would solve his temporary financial problems,
in the most benign way possible. He knew he would need
Chloe to be on board with the idea for it to have any chance of
working. Leaning into her back, Michael stroked her hair and
outlined everything.

A year of looking after the financials for Venetia Wright's
had shown him that £200,000 would not be missed. It could
be easily siphoned off to a different account that looked like
another arm of the charity. Michael proposed that he 'borrow'
this money and invest it. Within six months Michael knew
that he would be able to at least double the amount they'd
taken. At that point, the funds would be divided equally
between them all and the initial seed money returned to
Venetia Wright's account, its brief absence unnoticed. He
needed all of their signatures to siphon off this money. Venetia
had set up the directorships they held this way, so some
convincing was going to be required.

He knew Lucy desperately needed the money, and if
Chloe went along with the plan, she could be convinced. Nigel
seemed an easier prospect. Always desperate to be included,
they would make him feel like the lynchpin of the whole thing
— that his involvement was crucial for everyone else. And,

Michael pointed out to Chloe, not only would Venetia never miss this money, she was the kind of person who was constantly giving away her wealth. They were also deserving, weren't they? And besides, Michael told Chloe that with this investment in the stocks he had been careful watching for the last few weeks, he could slip the entire amount for all four of them back into the charity without anyone knowing. Chloe should think of this as a secret investment for Venetia's charity.

Chloe hadn't said anything that evening except that she'd think about it. But the next morning as they sat once more at the kitchen table, this time with Michael hurriedly scoffing down a piece of toast and checking his watch, needing to get home before Lottie and the boys, Chloe gave her answer.

'Okay,' she had said. 'I'll speak to Lucy about it before the next meeting.'

'And to Nigel as well?'

'Yes, I think with Nigel it would be better coming from me, too.'

Michael had stood up and moved over to embrace her. He thought perhaps he *could* walk away from his usual life for this woman. This woman who adored him.

What a difference eighteen months makes. The screaming and the crying when Michael had gently told Chloe that it was over. That he was going to try to make a go of it with his wife, for the sake of his family.

That is when she first threatened him.

'You can't leave me. How could you do this? I'll go to the police. I'll tell them everything that has happened.'

Michael hadn't taken this threat too seriously at the time — Chloe had a hell of a lot to lose, too. All four of them did.

But then another phone call came a couple of weeks later, with a slightly more sinister threat. One that he didn't tell the others about in the cafe this afternoon. Chloe revealed that she had gone to speak to Marcus Wright. Michael couldn't believe it — why would she do this? And that's when Chloe told Michael about her grand plan. She would speak to Detective Chief Inspector Luke Wiley, except he wasn't actually a detective anymore. He had royally cocked up Venetia's murder case and had left the force.

'Don't you see?' Chloe had said, her voice with a cruel edge he had never heard before. 'I'm going to go to him first. Tell him what happened that night. Tell him about the money. He, of all people, will understand a mistake. But it's up to me to say who was responsible for it all.'

And then the ultimatum. Go with Chloe to Detective Wiley and frame one of the others, tell him their guilt was too much to bear. Explain that they had moved the money, but it hadn't been their idea. And leave Lottie for her.

Or she would tell Wiley — and eventually the police — that he was responsible for absolutely everything.

'But why did you go to see Marcus? What on earth did he have to say for himself?' Michael had asked.

'He listened,' Chloe had said. 'He felt sorry for us. He said he understood. And he told me where to find Detective Wiley.'

This is the part of the conversation that he didn't relay to the others. He didn't tell them that when Chloe told him that Detective Wiley lived in a small village in the Cotswolds, he had scribbled down the address on a piece of paper, although he hadn't needed to in order to remember it. A simple house name, in a distinctively named village three hours outside of London. It couldn't be hard to find.

As Michael hurried home, he knew he had only one option if he was going to keep everything together. He had to finish what Chloe had started, which is what he should have done in the first place.

He pulled his phone out of his pocket and made the call.

'Nigel,' he said. 'I need a favour.'

TWENTY-TWO

As if it hadn't already been decided that Luke would speak to Marcus Wright, O'Donnell confirmed it.

He had barked down the hall from his office while Luke, Hana and Rowdy were still in conversation. As unpleasant as O'Donnell was, Luke knew that this was not the time to keep him waiting so he left the other two and made his way into the bowels of the Serious Crime unit.

Hackett was approaching from the opposite direction, having clearly just come from O'Donnell's office. He stopped and smiled at Luke, extending his hand.

'Good to see you back here, Luke,' he said.

'Thanks.'

Hackett nodded and continued down the hall, leaving Luke to the bad mood of their boss.

O'Donnell seemed to take great glee in informing Luke that he would have to interview Marcus Wright. He knew it would make Luke uncomfortable, which for him outweighed the embarrassment that his team had suffered during the murder case of Marcus's wife.

'He's not available until Monday, apparently,' O'Donnell said.

'Surely that's not ideal when we don't have a suspect yet for Chloe Little?'

'Not my call, Wiley.'

'Right. Anything else?'

Luke already had his back turned and was walking out the door back to his reclaimed office when the reply came.

'Yes. Don't fuck this one up.'

Luke bit the inside of his cheek and continued down the hall. For once, O'Donnell's comment was a fair one.

———

If he was being honest with himself, Luke was relieved to have a couple of days before he needed to speak to Marcus Wright, even if he was desperate to begin piecing this puzzle together. Hana had offered to come over and cook dinner for the two of them, or go out to see a film that evening, but Luke had graciously declined. This time was an opportunity to clear his head, a sensation he hadn't felt for the past fifteen months. The yoga classes he took now were really to fill his time, and because it was an activity that Sadie had loved. He simply took her place in the classes, as a sort of meditation to her memory.

But when he had been working, and especially on a difficult case, he needed time alone and he never did much in these hours. He cooked, he pottered, he let his subconscious do the rest of the work. He could do this anywhere, but he preferred to do it at Bluffs Cottage. If he quickly went home, picked up a couple of things and got straight in the car, he could be at the cottage by late afternoon. The traffic on the M40 motorway wouldn't be ideal, but that would just give him more time to think.

Sadie and Luke had bought Bluffs Cottage six months after they married. It had all happened quickly, and she had slightly bashfully admitted to Luke as they drove out to Gloucestershire that she had been wanting to buy a second home there for ages. So many of her London friends who began having kids in their late 20s and early 30s had toughed it out in the city with strollers and public transport and small flats with no garden for as long as they could until making the move to the countryside. Most of her gang had ended up in this very pretty part of England with its chocolate box houses and thatched roofs, the impressive stone Georgian design and its plethora of shops and food stores and pubs.

'The thing is,' Sadie said. 'I was just never going to do this alone.'

'I get it,' Luke said, reaching across to the passenger seat and squeezing her leg.

They had found the perfect house on the first visit, like it was fate.

'Please tell me you're not going to knock this down and redo everything,' Luke said, watching Sadie scanning the rooms, imagining that she was silently measuring and demolishing in her head.

'Are you kidding?' Sadie replied. 'It's gorgeous. I wouldn't change a thing.' She paused. 'Okay, maybe I'd put in a dishwasher.'

And that was all that they did. Bluffs Cottage was at the very end of a country lane and like the other half dozen houses on the lane it was light grey stone, with large windows on both stories, a small black pitched roof and two chimneys. One for the fireplaces that sat in the same position on different floors of the house — the drawing room and their bedroom, and the other for what used to be a wood burning oven in the country kitchen, but now filled by Sadie with white pillar candles.

In many ways it was the opposite of their London home, tiny in comparison with just four rooms downstairs and two bedrooms on the second floor. They had spent many happy weekends taking their time choosing rugs and coffee tables and light sconces. Luke had missed out on making the Arlington Square house into a home. He simply moved into something that Sadie had already created. This time, they were creating a home together and after Sadie died, Luke felt relieved that they had done this together. He wondered immediately after her death whether he would ever be able to set foot inside Bluffs Cottage again, especially considering how Sadie died.

The first time Luke returned to the cottage after Sadie's death, he had gone straight to bed and when he woke in the morning, felt the first seed of calm that he had experienced in weeks. As he stood in their kitchen that morning waiting for his coffee to brew, he realized that Sadie would have wanted him to continue his life in this cottage, in the home they were meant to be in together for the rest of the time they had on this earth. Except Sadie's time had been so cruelly taken from her. It had been taken from both of them.

———

Luke pulled up in front of his house in Arlington Square and parked on the 'No Parking' part of the street. He would only be a couple of minutes, needing just a change of clothes, his laptop and some coffee beans, unsure if there was coffee up at the cottage. He would throw them into the tote bag he was carrying and be on his way.

As he opened the front door, he could see the mail lying on the polished stone floor of the entrance hall. Except he had already picked up the mail that morning. He had heard it being delivered just before he left for the station. Perhaps it was an advertisement stuffed into an envelope.

Luke picked up the envelope and turned it over. **WILEY** was typed in a large, black font on the front. He put down the tote bag and opened the envelope. Inside was a single sheet of paper with one line in a large, typed black font.

STAY AWAY

Twenty-Three

The words were going through Nigel's head in a sort of chant. 'I hate them, I hate them.' Lucy and Michael hadn't seemed to be upset that Chloe was dead. And whatever Lucy was going on about in the cafe was inappropriate. He felt lonely and cheated and thought about his long dead mother. How her words were still in his head, too, all these years later. When Nigel would come home from school and his best friends had suddenly turned on him without warning, without reason, and he was left standing alone in the playground. He would hate them, too.

'You can't hate people just because they don't like you, Nigel. Try to be their friends. You have to work at friendships. That's how friendship works.'

That's how friendship works. Nigel shook his head as he descended the steps at Gloucester Road tube station to make his way back home. He couldn't get a seat, which annoyed him further, and as he jostled against people in the tube carriage, shopping bags rudely slung over their arms instead of at their feet, he closed his eyes and thought about who he hated more after that coffee.

Lucy, who should have known that Michael wasn't the only one who loved Chloe. He had a deep connection with her, too. Lucy, always so self-centred with her own problems, the way she pathologically played the victim, so constantly dull and wimpy and sullen. So unsuited to being an elementary school teacher, Nigel thought. Who was she inspiring? No one.

Or Michael, who had never really respected the contributions Nigel made to the committee. Just because he didn't work in *finance*, didn't mean he wasn't bringing knowledge of equal value. He certainly put in more time than Michael. He was the same as all of those dreadful alpha males with their slightly too tight trousers and expensive shoes. The way Michael had to lead a conversation, the way he raised his voice if he felt he wasn't being heard. Chloe had been taken in by this *spell* of Michael's and Nigel knew that if she just spent a bit of time with him, that she would come to her senses. She would see everything that Nigel had to offer. He swallowed and took a deep breath, thinking about how Chloe's hair used to fall in front of her eye and the way she ran her fingers through it as she tucked the strands back behind her ear.

He had wanted to spit out what he knew, but didn't trust them. That Chloe had called him, that she had asked him out for drinks and told him that they should go together to see Detective Wiley and implicate Michael as the architect of the whole mess and everything that happened afterwards. But part of the reason he didn't tell them the whole story was because he was still wounded by the conversation. He had tried not to think about it, it was better to not think about it.

He had been thrilled when Chloe had called. He knew that things had cooled with Michael and now, finally, she was seeing that Nigel was there, right in front of her, with so much to offer. He didn't mind that she probably guessed he liked her

— it would probably make moving forward together a little bit easier.

Nigel had even gone out and bought a new blazer. It was crisp and navy but the material felt so soft. And when he walked into the wine bar she had chosen in Fulham, Chloe had remarked upon it right away. Of course she had noticed something new about him. He had realized in that moment that she had been paying attention to him all along.

The first glass had been perfect. The conversation flowed, she had reached over and touched his arm. They had laughed. He couldn't even remember what they had chatted about, it all felt so natural. He knew he was probably glowing.

The evening began to sour with the second glass. At first, when Chloe asked him to come with her to speak to Detective Wiley, he was delighted. She was confiding in him, he thought they were connecting. But then her tone changed. The words coming out of her mouth were spiteful and dark. This was an act of revenge, and nothing more. She hadn't asked Nigel out after all. And worse, she was willing to sacrifice everything in order to get back at Michael.

Nigel had become very quiet at the table. He felt wounded, but desperately tried not to show it. He smiled at her and raised his eyebrows, trying to look as nonplussed as he could. He also had to think quickly — he realized that Chloe was suddenly becoming a loose cannon. One conversation between Chloe and Detective Wiley was all it would take. Nigel asked again where they would need to go to speak to the detective, then smiled and said he would think about it. Then he motioned to the waitress for the bill.

But now, as he thought about this evening, his tube carriage rumbled on, emerging from the darkness of the tunnel into the grey skies of the suburban west London. Nigel felt his phone vibrate in his pocket. He pulled it out to see Michael's name on the screen. He stared at the phone as it continued to buzz in his hand, watched it divert to voice mail, the missed call notification flashing onto the screen. He would need to deal with Michael eventually, but not now.

Nigel was not the sort of person to let his emotions get the best of him, but sometimes he felt overwhelmed. He felt almost close to tears by the time he entered his building, ascending the stairs to the upper floor and letting himself into his flat. The navy blazer, which was hanging on the back of his front door brushed against him as he shut it behind him. He grit his teeth and took off the jacket he was wearing, roughly hanging it on the hook so that it covered the blazer neatly on its hanger.

He poured himself a glass of water from the tap in the kitchen and stood in front of the refrigerator, staring at it. It was covered in pictures — some were photographs, others were clippings carefully cut out of newspapers, or images screenshotted from the internet and printed out onto paper. Each picture was of Nigel and various people from all of the volunteer groups he was a part of. There was the group from the 10K charity run where he handed out water, there was Nigel as the usher at a hospital fundraiser football game. There was the gang from the walking group on their trip to the York-shire Dales. And there was the picture of Venetia — she was standing in the middle of the four of them. It had been a glorious night, a black tie event for another charity that she ran, but she had invited them to it. Nigel had rented a tuxedo for the night and there he was standing next to Lucy. On the other side of Venetia were Chloe and Michael, his arm around her. The five of them beamed at the camera.

Nigel took the picture off the door, its little piece of white tack still stuck to the back. He pulled the pair of scissors out of the knife block on the kitchen counter, and cut the left third of the picture off. He watched the piece that held a smiling Michael float to the floor.

———

Lucy had been the first to get to Caffè Nero and the last to leave. She had been surprised that Nigel hadn't leapt in and also asked Michael exactly where he had been on Thursday night. She had thought he would have been more upset about Chloe's death, which made her wonder what exactly was going on.

She had been stunned that Chloe had told both Michael and Nigel about approaching Detective Wiley. So much for being such close friends.

'No, I'm sorry. This table is taken. I'm waiting for friends,' she said to the couple who asked if she was leaving.

Lucy then sat there for the next half an hour, not sipping another coffee, not looking at her phone. Just sitting there looking around at everyone else, taking up space, just because she could.

Twenty-Four

When they moved into Bluffs Cottage, the first thing that Sadie did after their dining room table had been delivered was invite the entire lane over for dinner. Ten people sat around the table, while Sadie spooned servings of steaming lamb curry into bowls and dolloped fresh yogurt on top. Crusty bread for dipping lay in the centre of the table and their guests seemed to find it charming to be invited to tear off hunks themselves.

The laughter around the table that night was a warm invitation into the community of this little neighbourhood in this tiny village in Gloucestershire. It also meant that Sadie enjoyed coming to the cottage on her own if Luke was working long hours on a case. She breezed into the homes of their neighbours for cups of tea and long chats, she traded garden saplings and was known for having a sixth sense about turning up to drop off something that had been borrowed just as a chilled bottle of wine was being opened.

Luke often would join this country life a day or so behind Sadie's arrival, taking the train out of London as soon as he could get out of the office. He entered the cottage one morning to find the school age children of one of their neighbours deep into an art project on their kitchen table, Sadie buzzing around them with crepe paper and sparkles and a glue gun. It was as if Luke had stepped into a vision of the life that was ahead of them, and he felt full with gratitude.

But today as he drove down the lane towards the cottage he had to mentally prepare himself for the fact that Sadie would not already be inside when he walked in the door. You could never truly prepare yourself for the waves of grief that came out of nowhere, sinking Luke even further below the water as if he was being held down by a riptide that he couldn't fight. It was so shocking to him still that Sadie was gone that he had to remind himself, like a timer he had to set to remember that she was truly absent from his life forever.

Luke's lovely neighbour Angus was close to the lane, clipping back a laurel hedge and he smiled and waved when he saw Luke's car. Luke slowed down and lowered the window.

'Hi, Angus. How are things?'

'Good! All is well! How are you doing? So great to see you here. Up for the whole weekend?'

All of their neighbours on the lane had been devastated by Sadie's death. He knew that. But they also went out of their way to accommodate Luke's grief by not showing it. He found them now friendlier than they had ever been, which charmed him and exhausted him in equal measure.

'A night or two. Believe it or not, I actually have a bit of work on at the moment.'

'Great!' Angus shouted through the window. 'Well, pop by anytime if you feel like you need a break. We're around. Or…I might just pop over myself with a nice bottle for some peace and quiet.'

Luke smiled. 'Sure, Angus. Anytime.'

When he entered the house, Luke thought he could still smell his wife. He lingered for a moment, breathing it in, before turning off the house alarm at the panel next to the front door. The four digit code was the day and month of their first date.

He walked through the house, checking each room to make sure that everything was okay. Nothing was out of place, nothing was leaking and Luke was pleased that he had clearly thought to stack firewood inside the house before he had left on his last visit. He wasn't sure it was enough to get him through the evening, but he'd make do for now as he felt weary from the drive and thinking about what Chloe Little had been wanting to tell him. Luke took a hot shower, threw on an old pair of sweatpants and decided to try reading a novel of Sadie's for awhile. Her collection of crime paperbacks was extensive, taking up an entire bookshelf in their drawing room. Sometimes he read something recent, although the accuracy of a police procedure could be really hit or miss, but he was quite taken with the older books with quirky retired detectives and grandparents who stumbled upon crimes and solved them. He used to joke that Sadie only married him because of her addiction to these books. *It certainly helped*, she had said.

When your loved one dies, it is difficult to sit in the space that they used to be in. Luke could never get his head around the feeling that she was still there, and yet would never be there again. He thought about Nicky's advice when he admitted how much he was struggling with it.

Sit with it. Sit with her. It is okay to feel she is still there.

Luke got up and padded into the kitchen to make himself a cup of jasmine tea. It was dark, the autumn evenings pulling in sooner now, and Luke looked out the French doors of his kitchen into the backyard. The only light came from the outside lanterns on Angus's back porch that gently filtered onto Luke's own small courtyard that ran off the kitchen. As he let the boiling water sit for a moment before pouring it over the tea leaves, Luke thought he saw something move just outside the door. His head snapped up and his eyes strained into the darkness. Luke kept very still, holding the kettle in his hand. He couldn't see anything and everything seemed still. A deer, probably.

Heading back to the drawing room, Luke tried to push the one memory in this house that he desperately wished he didn't have. That Marcus Wright had once sat in this very drawing room. Looking back at it all, Luke found it hard to believe. He would do anything to erase that this man had been here, the memory like a stain on one of the most precious places Luke had left in his life.

The day Luke had met Marcus Wright, when Marcus had waved off the victim support officers and asked Luke to stay with him just a little bit longer, he had been a completely shattered man. Luke remembered how his hand shook as he brought the glass of red wine to his lips and then he needed to use both hands to place the stemmed glass back onto the table in front of him.

Luke had been devastated for him. Marcus told Luke about Venetia, how she had suddenly appeared in his life and transformed it. How happy she made him, how incredible she was.

How could Luke not have understood this? How could he not have felt a connection between them? These were not questions that Nicky had posed later, when Luke sat in those first sessions with his therapist, reeling from everything that had happened in the months before. Nicky said these words aloud as statements of fact. They were meant to provide Luke with context, and perhaps with a little bit of comfort.

Luke had sat in the Wright's house for over three hours that evening. He had sat next to Marcus while Marcus scrolled through all of the photos on his phone, pointing out Venetia cooking in their kitchen, Venetia smiling at him on Christmas morning, the two of them at a cafe in Paris, his arm around the shoulders of his wife.

Luke had sat as silent witness to the sobs that had Marcus doubled over, hands gripping his knees, as shock and disbelief ricocheted through his body. *Oh my god, this could be me*, Luke had thought.

When he finally stood up to leave the Wright's home that evening, Luke had placed his hands on the shoulders of Marcus Wright and did something he never did with a family member of a victim. He made a promise.

'I will get whoever did this, Marcus. I promise you that.'

Marcus had welled up again and thanked him. Luke had gone home that night to Sadie and curled around her, already asleep in their bed.

———

At Bluffs Cottage it was getting late, but Luke didn't feel like going to bed quite yet. The firewood stack had dwindled so Luke pulled on a pair of battered trainers by the kitchen door and headed out to the log store that sat just beyond the small courtyard. It was colder than he thought and Luke shivered as he picked up a few logs and balanced them over his left arm. He was almost back at the house when he saw it. The figure was just a shadow reflected back in the glass of the kitchen door, which was still ajar.

A jolt of adrenaline surged through Luke as he realized he was not alone. He had been watched from outside the house and he knew immediately that he was in grave danger. Fear gripped him and he dropped the stack of wood, keeping just one log in his hand. The wood sliced into his hand as he gripped it.

But it was too late, he hadn't been able to move quickly enough. The man had his arm around Luke's neck, dragging him backwards and Luke gasped for breath. He needed to shout, he needed someone to hear him but all the came out was a garbled moan. Luke couldn't catch his breath. This man was trying to suffocate him.

Luke managed to twist violently enough to the right that he was able to break free and he desperately grabbed for the log, which had dropped to the ground. His hand was only grabbing fistfuls of air and he felt the man grab hold of him again.

It was then that Luke felt something crack into his ribs. The pain was utterly breathtaking as he felt his bones shatter. He shouted out. He couldn't breathe. Everything went dark.

TWENTY-FIVE

Lucy thought she was the kind of person who didn't care about money. Doesn't everybody think this? That their happiness is derived from simple pleasures — the small things like a good meal sitting in the sunshine, the joy of reading a great book, the company of friends and family.

But these were just platitudes, Lucy thought. Something to write on a dating profile, or to say to someone in order to sound well-rounded. Maybe, just maybe, they could be elements of happiness that you could aspire to achieve. But this was all easier said than done. How much easier would life be if you weren't worrying about the sudden rise in your electricity bill? Or the constant dread in the pit of your stomach that your landlord is suddenly going to decide to sell your flat and you will have to find another one. How lovely it would be to see a sweater you love in a store and simply decide to buy it right then and there, without even thinking about your bank balance. How different would your future look and how differently you would feel about it? Lucy imagined thinking about her future with pleasure, with anticipation of wonderful things ahead for her, instead of the haze of uncertainty she always felt.

Chloe hadn't thought about dropping the money to spend a couple of weeks in India. She wasn't the one working out tedious spreadsheets with a budget that accounted for every penny for months and months in order to be able to go. She hadn't squeezed the trip into a brief Easter break because she only had certain days of the year that she was able to take off.

Their unequal bank balances hadn't mattered when they were in India. Everything was so cheap and they happily split the cost of meals out and beers on the beach and a car and driver to visit the ancient forts. But when they got back to London, Lucy couldn't help but notice how different their lives really were. It didn't matter for the most part because their interests aligned and their conversations were the kind that went deep and long into the evening. Perhaps they were both the kind of person who didn't make friends all that easily and so the great fortune of meeting on a trip in a foreign country, realizing they lived in the same city, and getting on so fabulously, was not lost on either of them.

The two women were different in just one aspect. Their relationships with men. For once, Lucy felt like she had the upper hand here. Not in terms of being in a relationship, but in how she felt about herself. She dated off and on and was more than familiar with all of the online dating apps, but she felt that a partner would be additive to her life, not her entire reason for being.

Chloe, on the other hand, felt her single status was a giant personal failure. There was a part of Lucy that could understand this for her friend. Chloe seemingly had everything else, so why not this? She was beautiful, but more than that, she had the kind of body that effortlessly wore clothes well. Her hair was always lush and vibrant and she was clearly at ease with her physical self. She was intelligent and had worked very hard to achieve her position in her legal career, the money that came with it buying such a nice house close to the river in one of the loveliest parts of west London. She had interests that she had cultivated over many years — travel, photography, she was knowledgeable about contemporary art and often hopped on a flight to a myriad of European cities to check out an exhibition.

Frequently, after that extra glass of wine, Chloe would break down in front of Lucy. She would ask why she was alone, why didn't anyone want her? What was she doing wrong? Lucy could understand why her friend felt this way. When everything else was in place, you tended to focus on the one thing that was missing. Lucy could empathize with the loneliness, she also wanted to have someone sitting across the table from her over a lazy dinner at home instead of the heated up bowl of soup or pasta eaten on her lap in front of the television. But at the core of Chloe was something slightly different — it was a desperate need for her life to become complete. And only a man who fell in love with her and wanted the same things that she did would complete it.

Lucy's understanding of this hunger of Chloe's made her affair with Michael utterly predictable. Lucy hadn't particularly noticed that they had become close during all of those committee meetings. If there had been some sort of lingering glance or more attention paid to each other than to the rest of them, or a tactile gesture, Lucy had missed it.

And then Chloe purposely didn't tell her what was going on. Lucy had randomly seen them together. It had felt like a punch to the stomach. But more than that, she had felt an ache creep into her chest and settle there, a sensation that stroked her own loneliness.

She had been tutoring a student at the school at the end of the day and the session had gone quite late. It was a Friday evening and Lucy was tired. The week had been long and she had been looking forward to a quiet night before plans she had the following day for lunch with Chloe. At the exact moment that the bus stopped in traffic on Brompton Road, Lucy was wondering if she had any milk at home or if she needed to get off the bus one stop earlier to pick some up at the convenience store. Her brain was occupied by such a mundane thought that the sight of Michael and Chloe sitting in the window table in the wine bar was even more of a shock. Lucy initially felt a pang of being left out. Why hadn't they invited her out for some small plates and wine? Was her company not wanted? But then she suddenly and instantly understood what was happening.

Chloe had reached across and stroked Michael's face. He was laughing and then leaned in to kiss the spot just behind her right ear lobe. The bus began to move forward just as Chloe relaxed back into her chair, bringing her glass of red wine up to her lips. This movement looked like she had done it a thousand times before and Lucy knew that this date wasn't the first one. They were comfortable in each other's company. They were sitting in the window table of a bustling wine bar on one of the busiest streets in South Kensington on a Friday evening. This was all familiar to them.

The next day Chloe had said nothing. For a full three months, Chloe said nothing. Lucy couldn't believe it — if they were such close friends, why was Chloe keeping her affair a secret from her? She actually wasn't angry that Chloe hadn't told her. Instead, she was devastated. Their friendship had formed such a central part of her life and she wrestled with what felt worse: that she was suddenly the dreaded third wheel or that Chloe was purposefully withholding such a large part of her life from her. After three months, Chloe had asked Lucy over for dinner which is something that hadn't happened in several weeks. Lucy had wanted to decline, but beyond everything else, she missed her friend.

And then it all came pouring out of Chloe as soon as Lucy arrived.

'I'm so sorry I didn't tell you, Luce,' she said, gripping Lucy's arm. '

Please forgive me,' she pleaded. 'It's just that Michael's kids go to your school and you must see Lottie at the school gates all the time and Michael felt like he wanted to keep it all as locked down as possible. But finally I told him that you were one of my closest friends and if this relationship of ours was going to go anywhere, then you had to know.'

Lucy had felt like she had been chosen to keep this secret with Chloe and Michael and the last three months melted away. She wasn't a third wheel, she was now a purposefully included member of their group. Keeping their secret made her feel like she mattered deeply to them. She knew that she did.

That's when Chloe brought up Michael's grand plan. He would invest £200,000 of Venetia's money, double it within six months, and then cash all of them out before returning the initial sum to Venetia's bank account. Fifty thousand pounds was not a small amount of money. It would change her life.

But now Chloe was dead and she didn't trust Michael at all. Everything had fallen apart — the plan, their affair, and there was one other big problem. Lottie. What did she know? What had Michael told her?

It hadn't been easy to see her occasionally at the school gates during pick up time. Even though Michael and Lottie's boys were not in her class, the school was small and seeing Lottie was often unavoidable.

Lucy had asked Chloe where the £200,000 was and all she would say is that Michael was handling it through his account. That was a large sum of money to suddenly appear in a bank account. Did Lottie know? Was she a silent partner in this theft? Was it even her idea in the first place? How clever that would be, Lucy thought. To be pulling the strings of the theft but not being culpable at all? For a brief moment, Lucy wondered if that was all Chloe was to Michael. The pawn he needed as he set up the chess board of this scam — how else would he get Lucy and Nigel on side with taking this money? He needed her friendship with Chloe and he needed Nigel's infatuation with Chloe.

But what if Lottie didn't know? What if she had no idea that her husband was having an affair? All of those times Lucy had smiled and waved to Lottie at the school gates. The power she had to implode Lottie's life. But Lucy told herself that she was not that kind of person.

TWENTY-SIX

It took Luke a moment to understand where he was. He was very cold and one of his eyes wouldn't open. The stone tiles of the courtyard were sticky and he could smell pooling blood. It was his blood. His eyes began to sting as he blinked and realized that the reason he couldn't see out of one side was the blood that had settled over his eye. The left side of his body felt numb and he tried to move but his arm wouldn't bend without searing pain that shot up into his jaw.

Luke began to draw his knees towards his chest, a centimetre at a time, which is all he could manage as he winced and tried to draw in only short breaths.

He pressed down on his right foot and rotated just slightly until he thought he could maybe push himself into a seated position. He was unsure if his left side felt numb because he had been lying on it for who knows how long, or if there was severe damage.

A phone began to ring. Luke froze in place. Was he alone? Where was his attacker? His brain took an extraordinarily long time to understand that it was his ring tone. He moved his head to the left as far as he could and saw the phone screen lit up in the dark. The screen said HANA SAWATSKY. A small wave of relief rushed through Luke. She hated it when he didn't answer and would just keep calling. Sure enough, the phone went quiet and then immediately flashed bright again. The sound of the ringtone was so loud against the backdrop of the silent countryside.

'Luke?'

It was Angus, suddenly walking towards the courtyard from the front of the house. Angus stopped when he saw the phone lit up on the ground, not thinking to look past it to where Luke was lying.

'Angus,' Luke croaked.

The confusion on his neighbour's face change to horror when Angus finally saw Luke in the fetal position.

'Oh my god, oh my god.'

Angus rushed over to him, asking what had happened. Luke felt too exhausted to reply.

'I heard a noise and came outside and called for you. You didn't answer. Then I heard your phone ringing and ringing. Oh my god.'

'I think you just saved my life,' Luke whispered. 'Can you answer my phone and say that you are calling the police. It's just going to keep ringing otherwise.'

'What?' Angus asked.

But Luke simply closed his eyes and let everything fall into place around him, as he knew it would.

TWENTY-SEVEN

It was unusual, Hana knew, for a detective's partner to be such good friends with that detective's wife. When she looked back, Hana often couldn't remember who had entered her life first — Luke or Sadie. Sadie used to sometimes joke that it would just be easier if Hana moved into their house and while Hana had laughed, a little part of her ached. She loved that Sadie and Luke wanted her around so much, but she would have given a lot to have what they had. Life could feel quite lonely at times.

Losing Sadie had been excruciating for Hana. Not only did she lose one of her closest friends, she lost a big part of Luke in the process too. She had reacted by having an almost non-reaction. She put her head down at work, ground out the hours at the station and filled her off-time with anything physical she could think of. She was running the equivalent of a marathon each week and even this didn't exhaust her enough to sleep properly.

It is always on the most average of days when the worst possible things happen. Just over a year ago the Venetia Wright murder case had stalled — they still did not have a viable suspect. Two men had been cautioned and brought in for questioning. They thought they were close with one of them, but they had both been released without charge. They were at the stage where CCTV was being viewed a second and third time. Officers had been back out canvasing every shop and restaurant and train station for two dozen blocks around the crime scene. Luke and Hana had personally interviewed every single patron and staff member of the cocktail bar. And nothing. Luke had taken this lack of progress particularly badly. He had bonded with this bereaved husband over the six weeks that they had been hunting for Venetia's killer and was determined to not let the poor man down.

Hana felt that she needed the occasional break in order to see the case clearly. What were they missing? She had taken the Saturday off and she and Sadie had gone for a walk, done a bit of shopping and stopped for lunch. It had been the perfect late summer day — warm enough to sit outside and to want a bit of shade, but not too hot as to feel like the weather was an imposition in the course of their day.

Hana had thought about this lunch almost every single day since Sadie died. You never sit down for a lunch with your friend and think, *well, if this is the last meal we ever have together, I would like it to be like this.* But it had been, and if given the option of how it should be, the lunch was pretty near perfect. And Sadie had said something to Hana at the lunch that Hana knew she could never repeat again.

They had also talked about Marcus and Venetia Wright.

'Do you think you're getting any closer?' Sadie had asked. 'It's not that I'm worried about Luke, but he is not usually this preoccupied. It's just....taking up a lot of our lives at the moment. And I get it. Marcus is so lovely — Luke and I are both happy to be spending some time with him in the midst of all of this, but I don't know....'

Hana had shrugged her shoulders and brushed it off.

'Sometimes these cases are a little trickier and take a little longer. You know that,' Hana had said.

Sadie nodded and they continued their lunch. In fact, as Sadie's words had trailed off, Hana didn't know what to say in return. They weren't getting any closer and she wasn't liking how personally Luke was taking this case. He had gone from saying 'This could be me' to 'This would be me' — a subtle change in phrase that Hana realized wasn't subtle at all. Luke had shifted into a place where this tragedy that had happened to Marcus Wright was Luke's greatest fear acting out in real time in front of him.

And then, of course, his greatest fear became his unfathomable reality.

———

It was difficult to think about this entire day now. But it is all that Hana can think about after hearing that Luke had been attacked at Bluffs Cottage.

Hana had known immediately that something was wrong when Luke's neighbour answered Luke's phone after she had called it almost a dozen times. She spoke to him for only a few seconds, told him to call 999 and then began to make the calls herself. Luke's reinstatement to the force made getting every emergency service anywhere close to the cottage over there in just minutes. Hana didn't wait to hear which hospital he was being taken to, jumping in her car and beginning the three hour drive out to Gloucestershire, getting all of the information fed to her as she drove.

This was a drive that she used to enjoy, heading out to spend the weekend with Luke and Sadie in the countryside. But she hated it now. She hated the jumble of panic and dread that surged through her body as she negotiated the traffic coming out of London. She hated feeling like all of her senses were heightened as they can only be when you are suddenly in a situation that only previously existed as a dreadful hypothesis, something that you hoped would never actually happen to you.

She had felt all of this on that terrible day after lunch with Sadie. Less than twelve hours after their glorious lunch, she had made this exact drive. She played the events of that day over and over in her head. Where she was when she got the news, what she thought, how she felt, what she did next. She remembered sensations vividly — the way she had wrapped her arms around Luke, realizing that she never did this, how small his body felt to her as he began to shrink into his grief.

He had left the office only fifteen minutes or so before the phone call came in. She couldn't remember why. When she recounts every minute of what happened next, she is always grateful for this. Grateful that Luke wasn't still in Scotland Yard surrounded by colleagues when the call came in to say that his wife was dead.

She can't remember who patched the call through to her, but she does remember that she was distracted by something on her desk when the voice on the other end of the line informed her that Sadie Wiley's car had been seen partially submerged in the lake just off the A119 road past Barnsley and reported by a member of the public. Officers had called in the dive team who had found Sadie still strapped in the driver's seat. She remembers that the word 'lucky' had been used. They were lucky that the divers had arrived at the tail end of dusk, or searching the car may have had to wait.

Hana had frozen in place, her mouth instantly dry but sweat began to form on the rest of her. She felt very cold. Hana asked the caller to identify themselves as she hadn't really been listening and her first thought was that this was an error — something meant for another department, another person, someone else's tragic news that couldn't possibly be meant for them.

This cannot be happening.

By the time the details were spoken again and Hana hung up, word had circulated through the entire office floor. When Hana stood up from her desk, every single one of her colleagues was standing as well. A symbolic sign of respect and understanding of the gravity of what had just happened. Even O'Donnell looked pale.

'Where is he?' O'Donnell asked.

'Home.'

'Which home?'

'London.'

Hana had looked around at the contents of her desk, picking up papers that she thought she might need if she was to be away for a few days. Then she realized that what she was doing was ridiculous. She wouldn't be doing anything at all.

Hana grabbed her bag and began to walk towards the elevator as everyone stared at her, in silence. She needed to get to Luke. She needed to get there before anyone else did.

O'Donnell followed her down the hallway.

'Take officers with you.'

'No.'

'Sawatsky. Take some support. Let me drive you.'

Hana stopped short and turned to face O'Donnell. She didn't refuse again, she didn't say anything at all.

O'Donnell took a step back and nodded.

―――――

How do you tell someone that the person they love the most in the world is dead? Hana spent twenty minutes thinking about it as she made her way to Arlington Square. Every minute felt double the length of time and she felt desperate.

She simultaneously wanted to get there as quickly as possible and yet was acutely aware that Luke was living the last minutes of a life that would never be the same again. Hana was about to shatter it.

She doesn't remember exactly what she said, or how she said it. She remembers that she didn't wait to go inside. Hana told Luke what had happened standing right there on the doorstep of the house that Sadie had lovingly and painstakingly built.

Hana does remember what happened next.

Luke was quiet for a moment, his brain taking in this information but not yet understanding it. And then he began to scream.

Hana let him.

———

Hana's tears came only as Luke went inside to get his phone. She realized that Luke was calling Sadie.

It went straight to voicemail.

Luke lowered the phone from his ear, as if he was moving in slow motion. He stared at the screen, the call still connected to the messaging service. Hana thought about that message which would have been recorded on Sadie's voice mail. The empty space lingering there, the void that death brings for everyone left behind.

'Where is she?' Luke asked.

'She was taken to the coroner in Gloucester. But we have arranged for her to be brought back to the coroner here. Dr. Chung will do it. If you want.'

Luke was quiet for a moment and then felt in his pocket for his keys. He turned to shut the front door and locked it.

'I need to get to her.'

'I can't imagine that she will be brought back to London tonight, Luke. It will probably be in the morning.'

Luke began to sob, his hands grasping at the air, grabbing onto nothing. Hana put her arms around him and he whispered, 'I have to get to my wife.'

What else was there to do? So Hana got Luke settled in the passenger seat of her car and began to drive the three hours out to the coroner in Gloucester. They drove in silence. When they arrived, Luke thanked her, speaking for the first time since he last uttered those words on his front steps, and went inside.

Hana sat in her car in the pitch darkness, almost paralyzed. How could she leave her partner and the body of her best friend? She sat in the car for almost an hour, watching over the coroner's building like some sort of guardian, or at least as an acknowledgment of the horror of what was happening to them.

Eventually, the coroner van pulled around from the back of the building and she watched Luke walk out to it and get into the front passenger seat.

Hana started the engine and began the three hour journey back to London, following Luke and the body of his wife the entire way. A funeral cortege only understood by the two of them.

Twenty-Eight

When Hana arrived at Gloucester General Hospital, she was directed to fifth floor and was relieved that it was not the intensive care floor. She also extremely relieved to see the police protection unit standing outside Luke's room.

She flashed her ID at the officers and was let inside. Luke was awake and chatting to one of the nurses.

'Hana. Hey. You didn't need to drive all the way out here.'

'No,' Hana said. 'I just thought I'd hang out at home when someone tried to kill you.'

Luke chuckled and then immediately winced. The nurse looked at Hana and shook her head.

'You're not going to want to make him laugh for awhile,' she said. 'Two broken ribs. Not terribly comfortable.'

'Shit,' Hana said. 'Sorry. How is everything else?' She pointed at him.

'Concussion, contusions, and one broken collarbone. Again, not terribly comfortable,' said the nurse.

'I'm fine, Hana,' Luke said, trying to be reassuring. Hana let herself feel reassured.

'I haven't spoken to the officers yet, so do you want to fill me in?'

Hana pulled up a chair next to the hospital bed.

'He just came out of nowhere. But he was waiting. I went outside to get some firewood and he was on me in under a second. I'm guessing that he'd been watching me in the house for awhile.'

'Jesus,' Hana said.

'There's something else.'

When Luke told her about the envelope that had been pushed through his letterbox in London, she was less than impressed.

'Why didn't you call me immediately? Is it still there? We need forensics on it.'

'Yes,' Luke said. 'I left it inside the house. We can get it when we're back in London.'

Hana looked at her watch.

'When are they discharging you?'

'I'm waiting for the on-call doctor to sign me out, but it should be soon. I need to go back to the cottage to get some things and properly lock up. But then we can go.'

'And maybe thank your neighbour?'

'Yes,' Luke said. 'We can pick up a good bottle for Angus on our way back.'

Hana and Luke went over everything in detail again. She asked him to recount every moment of the day leading up to the attack.

'What's your instinct?' Hana said.

'Honestly, I don't know,' Luke replied. 'It's not random, obviously. My guess is that someone thinks Chloe Little did tell me something before she died.'

'Something worth killing for.'

'Killing Chloe and then killing me. Yes.'

'Well, my next question then is…who else knows? Who else has this information? Who's next?'

TWENTY-NINE

L uke should have perhaps called Nicky Bowman first before turning up at her door with his face looking like it did and his arm in a sling. Her mouth dropped open and she stood there, not moving.

'I think this is where I'm supposed to say, you should see the other guy.'

'Luke. Oh my god.'

'I'm fine, really.'

Nicky realized she was blocking the door, muttered 'sorry' under her breath and then ushered Luke inside.

'Have you been to the hospital?'

'Oh yes,' Luke smiled.

'Was there another guy?'

Luke laughed, he couldn't help it, but the pain in his broken rib stopped him short. He took a sharp breath and leaned against the wall in Nicky's entranceway.

'Do you want me to help you upstairs?' Nicky asked.

'No, no. I'm fine. Thanks.'

Luke gingerly followed his therapist up the stairs, Nicky turning around every few steps to check on him.

It felt like such a relief to Luke to be sitting in his usual spot on the comfortable leather sofa in his therapist's office. Nicky's calm presence sitting opposite him, the light that always seemed gentle in this room from the windows to his left. As he began to relax, his body began to ache.

'I'm guessing there's quite a story here?' Nicky said.

'You could say that.'

Luke filled her in, leaving out the explicit details of what happened to him in garden of Bluffs Cottage. It was clear enough from his face what had occurred. When he was finished, Nicky didn't say anything. As was often the case, she opened up a space for Luke to continue talking. They sat in silence for a minute.

'Luke, this is quite serious.'

'In what way?' he asked.

'In the way that someone tried to kill you,' Nicky said.

He knew that he would have to reassure Nicky and explained the police involvement and that they would soon know who did this. And that Luke was perfectly safe.

'Right,' Nicky said. 'Except I can't help but think that maybe this wouldn't have happened if you had let one of your colleagues know about the letter that was anonymously posted through your door.'

'Yes,' Luke chuckled. 'That's exactly what Hana said.'

Nicky took a deep breath and looked at Luke. She was trying to not feel overcome with concern for her client. She was trying to focus on how she could help him when so much of this situation was out of her hands. She felt responsible for Luke's emotional world, but how does she explore that with him when there was someone trying to kill him?

'What are you thinking?' Luke asked her, the silence between them extending a beat or two longer than usual.

'Honestly? That therapists aren't exactly trained for this.'

Luke held onto his side with the one hand that wasn't suspended in the sling as he laughed.

'Yeah, sorry about that.'

Nicky smiled at him. He wondered what she was thinking, what she wasn't ever going to say to him.

'Well,' she said. 'I think we should start with how you're feeling about this. I mean, the last time you were here you were debating with yourself whether or not you wanted to get involved in this case. Another murdered woman, and with an element of something very personal added into the mix yet again. Do you know yet why she had the photo of you on her when she died?'

'Okay,' Luke said. 'That's kind of a two part question so I have a two part answer.'

'Shoot.'

'With a caveat that you're not going to like the second part of the answer.'

Nicky raised her eyebrows. 'Okay. I'm intrigued.'

'Right,' Luke sat forward on the couch. 'Apart from feeling physically...not great, I feel okay. There's a part of me that, I guess, missed being at work. Being with Hana feels good, walking into Scotland Yard feels good — and I wasn't sure that it would — so all in all, I'm okay.'

'And the second part?' Nicky asked.

'We think we know why Chloe Little had a photograph of me. She was trying to speak to me. She was...seeking me out to tell me something.'

'To tell you what?'

'That we don't know.'

'Okay,' said Nicky. 'But do you know why she wanted to speak to you specifically?'

'We believe so.' Luke paused, unsure of exactly how to say what he had to say next. He looked straight at Nicky as he said it, almost as if she was a suspect that he was examining for a specific reaction. As if she would have the answer to all of the questions swirling around in his head.

'We believe that she had spoken to Marcus Wright. Marcus told her to find me.'

'Oh my god,' Nicky said, any semblance of therapist professionalism wiped from her face completely.

————

When Luke turned up at the door of Dr. Nicky Bowman all those months ago at Hana's insistence, in the first session he told her, through the quiet sobs of a man in an ocean of grief, about the day of Sadie's death. In the second session he told her about the day Marcus Wright had come to stay with Luke and Sadie at Bluffs Cottage.

Sadie had been unimpressed.

When Luke hung up the phone on that Friday morning from his call with Marcus —the regular check-in call, letting him know the progress of the case and if anything new had cropped up the previous day — he mentioned to Sadie that he had told Marcus they would be in the country for the weekend and if he was at a loose end, he should think about coming for a night.

'You didn't think that I should have been consulted about this?' Sadie said. 'God, Luke. It's one thing for you to feel so involved in this case and with this man. But this is our home.'

Luke apologized, and really he should have checked in first, he knew that. But Marcus had been in tears again on the phone and he offered the invitation more as a gesture than anything else. It was unlikely that he would drive all the way out to the Cotswolds to have dinner with them.

Except that he did.

Marcus turned up on Saturday afternoon with two excellent bottles — a champagne and a California white — and a stunning bundle of hyacinths and lilies. Sadie was polite, but Luke knew she was irritated, and the three of them sat outside in the little courtyard soaking up the last sunny afternoons of September.

Marcus went out of his way to not be in the way. He offered to help Sadie peel vegetables for their dinner, he helped Luke re-affix the trellis at the back of the garden that had blown over in a recent windstorm. He fit into their Saturday with ease, suggesting a cheeky glass of wine in between tasks as they relaxed and chatted. Luke watched Sadie laugh at Marcus's jokes and the day quickly felt like they had a friend over from a neighbouring house, not the bereaved husband of a murder victim of a case Luke couldn't solve who had imposed himself on their weekend.

Luke felt relieved, and as usual he enjoyed Marcus's company. The three of them had a lot to talk about — common travel stories, similar interests in books and film, familiar personal stories of meeting their spouse a little later in life.

Venetia was part of the evening in this way. It was almost as if she was travelling, or simply away somewhere for awhile, but that Luke and Sadie would properly meet her when she returned. How easy it was to slip into this falsehood. Sadie said after Marcus left the following morning that she had caught herself remembering that Venetia was dead and actually felt winded by it. Luke had nodded and kissed her, acutely aware of the identical sensation and in gratitude for his wife who empathized with others so deeply.

Sadie had gently asked Marcus about Venetia over dinner. It felt like their afternoon had opened a door into a world they could now speak about. They could tell that Marcus was immediately grateful to speak about her. How lonely he must have felt to have Venetia ripped out of his life but then to have the added weight of feeling like he couldn't keep talking about his dead wife for fear of people becoming tired of hearing about it. But for Sadie, all of this was new. And for Luke, as he was about to discover, so much of it was new to him too.

Marcus had suffered a lonely childhood. His dad was not the nicest of dads and wasn't what you would call a warm or affectionate person. Sadie and Luke had read between the lines as Marcus described him. But his mother was just the opposite. She had been a calm and joyful presence in his life. Always there, always supporting him, tremendous fun. There had been so much laughter with her in the house when it was just the three of them - Marcus, his mother, and Marcus's younger brother.

'We called ourselves The Three Musketeers,' Marcus had said, beaming at Sadie and Luke.

But then his mother got sick. Breast cancer. It all went downhill very quickly and Marcus was only twelve years old. His mother had tried to protect her boys from her illness, but Marcus knew that something serious was happening. She was away in the hospital, and then so sick when she got home. He remembered her wig wasn't quite the right colour and she never looked like herself in it, her body getting thinner by the day, the grip of her arms that still wrapped themselves around him any moment she could feeling weaker and weaker.

Marcus became very quiet at the table in Bluffs Cottage as he spoke about his mother's death. He had been in the room with her alone. He knew that she had slipped away but couldn't really believe it. How do you understand what is happening in that moment, especially when you are twelve years old? Marcus had reached out to hold her hand, thinking that for the first time as he was growing into a young man and she had become so frail and tiny in her illness, that her hand fit neatly into his. It had been warm and he was comforted by that, like she would always be with him even in death. He needed to get his little brother so that Tom could be able to have this, too.

Tom was asleep in the room that the boys shared and Marcus gently woke him up. He was a perceptive boy for at just ten years old — he knew immediately that something was wrong even before Marcus told him. Marcus remembered how Tom had buried his small head into his neck and had folded himself into Marcus, his breath hot on his collarbone, his body shaking every few breaths as he sobbed in silence. Marcus hadn't needed to say a word to his brother, but just held him for a few minutes.

When Marcus lifted Tom up, he put his arm around his shoulders and picked up the little stuffed lion, now well-loved and squashed, its fur pilled and patchy in places, and brought it with them. As he held the soft toy in his hand, Marcus thought about his father ridiculing Tom for still having it, so cruel in his taunting that created the need for his brother to want the lion with him in his bed in the first place. Tom had looked towards the closed door of their parents' bedroom, their father asleep inside it as their mother now lay dead in the guest room. He steered his brother past it and they crept down the hall together.

Marcus led Tom into the room and quietly shut the door behind him, wanting this private space for the three of them. He thought Tom would be anxious or scared but instead his brother slowly walked up to their mother and stared at her. Marcus wondered if he was silently saying a prayer.

After another minute had passed, Marcus sat on the very edge of the bed where he had been sitting before and picked up his mother's hand again. This time it was cold and lifeless. Marcus had choked on his breath and Tom had looked at him, alarmed. But Marcus smiled at his brother and motioned for him to come and sit in his lap. Marcus held his dead mother's hand, trying to make it warm one more time. He took Tom's hand, still the hand of a small boy, and placed it on top of his own. The boys held onto their mother this way for a long time, saying a quiet goodbye, Marcus promising himself in that moment to always shield his brother. Nothing would ever hurt this little boy again. It was the last thing he whispered to their mother before he left the room, knowing he would never see her again.

It is sometimes easy to look at a singular moment in time and understand that it is the worst moment of your life. It is harder to absorb that what can come afterwards in a slow dripping of residual pain is so much harder. This is what happened to Marcus over the next couple of months and focusing on his brother and his well-being was the life raft that kept him afloat. But everything would be torn apart as the end of that summer approached. Their father had found looking after two young boys by himself intolerable. The easiest solution was boarding school. Marcus had overheard the one-sided telephone conversation about term times and uniform requirements. He had seen the large, stiff envelopes with mysterious crested emblems on the top left corner and wondered which school it was. Where would they be going? What would it be like? He desperately missed his mother.

It had been a shock to hear that he was not going anywhere. It was explained to him not gently, or with any soft apology, but plainly and unemotionally with a shrug of his father's shoulders. There wasn't enough money to send both brothers to boarding school. Marcus was about to turn thirteen, he had missed the cutoff for the first year of senior school already, so what was the point? It was Tom who was the perfect age to start anew and off he would go to a better place, a brighter future, the safety of being away from this dreadful house.

The boys were inconsolable about being separated and Marcus told Luke and Sadie how he marked each day off on a calendar he had hidden in his desk drawer. He and Tom were desperate for summer to arrive so they could be together again. When it did finally arrive and Tom returned home, he was a good foot taller and the small hand that Marcus had held over his own and his mother's, was big and tanned and no longer fit in his pockets, though he tried to stuff them in there in his usual way.

But Marcus was bigger too — he had spent as much of the year out of the house as possible — mostly on runs that would pass for half marathons, and lifting makeshift weights. He wouldn't be pushed around again and made sure of it.

His long runs had brought him a most welcome discovery. Ten miles or so into the countryside from their house was a pond. At first Marcus thought it was an abandoned quarry, but it was filled with water that was just deep enough to swim in and never seemed to evaporate. The water table must have been very high here and the pond felt like a miracle — like magic appearing in front of him. The woods that surrounded the pond were close enough that Marcus tied a rope to a sturdy branch on the tree closest to the east side of the pond and with a bit of effort, could make it swing far enough to jump off into the middle of the pond. It was glorious and this activity would take no effort at all when there were two of them. One to swing the other, no need for pumping legs and tired biceps trying to cling on for long enough before releasing into the water. Marcus couldn't wait to show Tom.

And Tom absolutely loved it. It became their daily routine that summer, like they were characters in a novel — young boys on an adventure. Tom's voice had just begun to break and Marcus would gently tease him about it, making Tom blush in front of his older brother that he desperately wanted to impress.

One afternoon, everything went wrong. They had only been at the swimming pond for five minutes, maybe less, and the run out from the house had made them tired on an especially hot day. It was humid in the way that summer rarely catches on in England during the summer months. Both boys had already jumped into the pond to cool off and Marcus was lying out under the tree that held the rope swing, resting. The sun was blazing down and he remembered holding his hand in front of his face, his fingers together as he tried to use his flat palm as a shade.

Tom climbed into the tree a second time and asked Marcus to pull him back on the swing so he did and then settled back onto the grass as he heard the splash in the water. After a few seconds Marcus realized that he heard nothing. He sat up and scanned the pond, assuming he would see his brother quietly swimming to the side. But the water was flat and calm. Marcus stood up and scanned the water again. Was his brother playing a trick on him, pretending to still be under the water? Marcus called for Tom. Nothing.

Panic began to rise in his throat and he walked quickly towards the pond edge. He called again. He scanned the pond again. The pond was small, where was he? Marcus stood at the edge for one more second before diving into the water. He swam into the middle of the pond but couldn't see anything and then suddenly his leg brushed against something. He dove down and pulled Tom up. He wasn't breathing. How heavy Tom was as Marcus dragged him to the edge of the pond, how hard it was to pull him over the edge. He was just about to turn thirteen years old. He didn't know how to resuscitate someone but he tried. And he tried and he tried.

Marcus sat next to his brother's body. He reached for Tom's hand, which was as cold as his mother's was on that night. Marcus didn't want to leave him there, but he had to find someone to tell and so he left.

At the dining table in Bluffs Cottage, all three of them were very quiet as Marcus got to this point of his story. Sadie had brushed away tears that had slipped down both cheeks. The story was finished. There was simply nothing else to say.

Luke had reached over and gripped Marcus's shoulder, squeezing it every so slightly. Marcus had then apologized to both of them for going on for so long, for telling this sad story at such a lovely dinner. He apologized for being a terrible guest.

'Don't be silly,' Sadie said.

'Venetia walking into my life changed everything.'

'I can imagine.'

'I couldn't believe that I told her about Tom so soon after meeting her. It's just not something I tell many people,' Marcus said. 'That's how I knew that we were going to be together for a long time. I just knew.'

'I'm so sorry, Marcus,' Luke said.

'You know, it's funny. Venetia grew up with all of her money — it was family money — and she was casual about it. I mean, not reckless or that she wasn't grateful for it, but she made sure that it didn't define her.'

'I can understand that,' Sadie said and Luke knew that she really did understand.

'Venetia said that if we had children, they would never be separated like Tom and I were. That our money could at least do that.'

'That's a nice thing, a comforting thing to say to you,' Sadie gestured.

'I suppose,' said Marcus. 'But money can't protect you from death.'

THIRTY

When Luke walked out of Nicky's house, he was no closer to reconciling a face to face meeting with Marcus Wright who he had not seen in over a year. Nicky was never going to give him advice — it wasn't her role as his therapist, but he could tell that she thought it was a terrible idea.

Luke noticed Hana's car parked across the street before she had noticed him walking towards it. He knocked on her window. Hana started the car engine and lowered the glass.

'I'm loving my new car and driver service,' Luke said.

'Ha ha. Get in.'

'How did you know that I didn't drive here?' Luke asked as he sat down in the car and fastened his seatbelt.

'Even with your injuries, I know you like the walk. How are you feeling?'

'Like shit, thank you.'

'Great. Let's go.'

Hana pulled out of her parking spot and did an illegal u-turn on the street as Luke checked his phone.

'There's a missed call from Rowdy.'

'Yep, we're heading to the station. We have arrested Nigel Quail.'

Luke looked surprised. 'Nigel Quail? For Chloe's murder?'

'No,' Hana replied. 'For your attempted murder.'

'You're kidding.'

'That's just what you want a senior detective to say when we've arrested someone. *You're kidding.*'

Luke bit the inside of his cheek and touched his aching ribs.

'Okay, so what do we have?'

'Ah, let's let Rowdy fill you in. She's missed you.'

———

When the elevator doors opened on the seventh floor of Scotland Yard, Rowdy was hovering by the elevator. Her smile quickly faded when she saw Luke.

'Oh god. The bastard. Are you alright? I bet you didn't put anything on that eye.'

'I'm okay, Rowdy,' Luke said as he put his one good arm around her shoulders.

'Well, come and sit down. Let me show you what we've got. And you have your brilliant partner to thank for this.'

Luke turned to Hana and raised his eyebrows.

She shrugged.

'Never lead with the best part,' Hana offered.

The three of them sat down in Luke's old office, which Luke supposed was temporarily his again. Rowdy had the laptop open and waiting for them.

'Hana asked me to get the license plates of all three of the remaining committee members. Lucy Bishop doesn't own a car but Michael McPherson and Nigel Quail do. It took awhile to get the Automatic License Plate Recognition data in, but then we got him. We got him heading out to your village on the M40 and we've got him coming back in on the M4 almost eight hours later. Not only that, we've got him smack in the middle of your village on a doorbell camera. You have the local officers to thank for that. They were not particularly pleased to have a detective attacked on their patch.'

'And it's Nigel Quail's car?' Luke said.

'The one and only,' Rowdy replied.

'What?' Hana asked. 'This doesn't feel right to you?'

'I don't know, Hana. It's hard to say what feels right or doesn't feel right. It happened very quickly. I mean, I've never seen this guy. Hackett and Smith did that interview. Does it fit to you?'

Hana shrugged her shoulders.

'We have his car multiple times, Luke. It would be a pretty big coincidence that he just happened to be on a jolly on that one particular day in that very specific part of the Cotswolds where you were attacked.'

'I saw him come in, Luke. He was pretty average in size,' Rowdy said. 'What sort of size did your attacker seem?'

'Pretty goddamn big.'

'Look,' Hana said. 'I picked you up because Hackett and Smith are waiting to do the interview. They obviously wanted to give you first dibs here if you want to go in.'

Luke said he'd go and speak to Hackett and Smith first and went down the hall in search of them.

Rowdy took this opportunity to speak to Hana.

'How is he, Hana? Is this all too soon?'

Hana didn't know how to answer. Partly because she didn't know the answer and partly because she knew that they were both about to lie to each other.

'I don't know,' she said. 'He seems okay to me. Doesn't it feel good to have him back here?'

'Of course it does,' Rowdy said. 'I can't help but worry about him. But he seems okay.'

The two women stood there in a silence they both didn't need to fill.

———

Hackett and Smith had no trouble with Nigel Quail when they turned up at his flat. He seemed surprised to see them, and invited them inside.

When he was asked for his whereabouts the previous day, Nigel began to look uncomfortable.

'I was here. At home.'

'All day and into the evening? You didn't go out anywhere?' Hackett asked.

When they asked Nigel to voluntarily accompany them to the station for further questioning, he said that he would be happy to pop down there in a couple of hours. That he had to make some calls and do some errands first.

At that point, the detectives arrested him for the attempted murder of Detective Chief Inspector Luke Wiley. Nigel hadn't said a word since.

Luke looked at Nigel through the two-sided glass. He looked calmer than he should be in this circumstance and was sipping a paper cup of hot tea. The only sign of any encroaching anxiety was the way he kept pushing his glasses back up his nose, as if he was sweating.

'He hasn't asked for a solicitor, although we have, of course, given him this option,' Smith said.

'Would you like to speak to him first, Luke?'

Luke shook his head. He preferred to watch the interview where he could look for any sort of clue as to what the hell was going on without being distracted by his own line of questioning. He also did not confess to Hackett that he felt more than a little out of practice.

Luke watched Hackett and Smith sit down across the small table from Nigel Quail and turn on their digital recorder. Nigel once again waived the right to have a solicitor present for the interview. Then he put down his paper cup of tea and leaned forward in his chair.

'I can give you everything you need,' Nigel said.

'How is that?' Smith asked.

'I can tell you who killed Chloe Little.'

Luke knew watching through the glass that Hackett and Smith would have done everything in their power to refrain from looking at each other in that moment.

'You know who killed Chloe Little.' Smith said this as a statement of fact with a hint of surprise.

'I do,' Nigel repeated.

'And you didn't wish to tell us this before when we interviewed you at your home?'

'I apologize unreservedly for that,' Nigel said. 'I was protecting someone but I know that was wrong and I am here to give you all of the information that you may need.'

At this point, Hackett turned around and looked towards Luke, as if to say through the glass: *What the hell is going on here?*

'Why don't you fill us in then, Mr. Quail,' Smith gestured.

'Michael McPherson killed Chloe. I am sure of it. And he took my car yesterday and I understand that something happened to Detective Wiley. I hope very much that he is alright.'

This was all quite unexpected and Hackett and Smith weren't sure what they were dealing with. Was this guy a little crazy? Was he actually the culprit and was framing another member? Or was he just stringing them along for his own amusement?

'Why don't you tell us everything you know, Mr. Quail. And start from the beginning.'

It was at this point that Luke and Hana pulled up two chairs and took a seat on the other side of the glass.

Thirty-One

When Michael's name flashed onto Lucy's phone screen, she really didn't want to answer it. She was on her lunch break at school on what was already a very tiring Monday and honestly could Michael just leave her alone.

'What do you want Michael?' she snapped.

'I'm sorry to bother you in the middle of the day, but have you spoken to Nigel?'

'Why are you asking?'

'I spoke to him yesterday and he sounded a little bit off. I've just tried him again now and he's not picking up.'

Lucy wondered what this was about — it would be like Michael to try to get information out of her. What did he want to know?

'Can I ask you a question, Michael?'

'Uh, okay.'

'What exactly does Lottie know?'

There was a long pause on the line.

'What do you mean?' Michael asked.

'I mean just what I said. What exactly does she know?'

'She knows nothing! Why are you asking me this? Of course Lottie doesn't know anything.'

Lucy didn't say anything.

'Lucy!' Michael was hissing now. 'What are you on about? Have you spoken to Nigel or not?'

'Wouldn't you like to know,' Lucy said, before pressing her finger hard onto the end call button.

———

Michael wasn't one to panic, but he was beginning to feel like everything was spiralling out of control, or at least out of *his* control. Why was Lucy being so obstinate? This wasn't like her — she was usually the one who just went along with things. She was the dependable quiet one of the four of them.

Clearly, Michael thought, she has spoken to Nigel. He could deal with that, but the more pressing concern was that she may have also spoken to Lottie. This was the last thing he needed.

———

The one person who wasn't panicking was Nigel. He was quite the opposite and calmly moved his cup of tea to the side, folding his hands together and placing them on the table in front of him.

'You are going to want to take this all down,' he said to Hackett and Smith, as if waiting for them to immediately summon notebooks and pens to the interview room.

Smith pointed at the recorder on the table and told Nigel that everything was being thoroughly taken down.

'It all began last year,' Nigel said. 'This was before Venetia was killed. Chloe came to me first — I'm the most integral part of our committee — and suggested that the committee borrow some money from Venetia's charity fund.'

'Borrow some money?' Hackett said.

'Yes, that's right. I know now that this was all Michael's idea. He thought that he could move £200,000 out of the fund and distribute it equally between the four of us. We could then do what we wished with the money.'

'This money that you stole from Venetia Wright?'

'Well,' Nigel bristled slightly, 'It was more of an investment idea at the time. I wasn't sure what I was going to do with my portion. I was perhaps going to donate it to another of the charities I'm involved with. I do a lot of volunteer work with for so many worthy causes. I'm sure you already knew that.'

Hackett looked bemused.

'So what did you do with the money?' he asked.

'We still have it. That's the point. We all still have the money, so *in effect*, nothing has been taken from Venetia at all.'

Nigel looked triumphant and leaned back in his chair.

'I'm sorry,' Hackett said. 'But I'm not quite following. The four of you stole £200,000 from Venetia Wright and the money is still just sitting there in one of your bank accounts not being spent?'

'Correct.'

'Why on earth not?' Smith ventured.

'Because Venetia died. She was *murdered*. It was absolutely not appropriate to do anything further with the money.'

'I'm sorry,' Hackett said one more time. 'Let me get this straight. The four of you stole Venetia's money but then had a change of heart after she died when your conscience kicked in? Am I getting this right?'

'Well, not exactly. But this isn't really the point,' Nigel said, sounding more and more exasperated.

'Okay. What does this have to do with the murder of Chloe Little?' Smith asked.

'That's what I'm getting to — but you need to have the background *first*,' Nigel said.

Hackett and Smith couldn't get over this guy, sitting in front of them under arrest, seemingly oblivious to the severity of the situation and thinking he was in charge of this increasingly bizarre conversation.

'You see,' Nigel continued. 'Chloe and Michael were having an affair.'

The detectives looked at him blankly.

'Don't you get it?' said Nigel. 'Michael ended the affair and Chloe was very upset. I believe that she threatened to tell the police about the money so Michael must have killed her.'

'And you're just telling us now?'

'Well, it's only just clicked with me now. You came to arrest me for the attempted murder of a detective. You can't imagine my shock when you turned up at my flat. But I know that Michael was responsible for this, too.'

'And how do you know that?' Hackett asked.

'Because Michael called me yesterday and asked if he could borrow my car. He said that his wife was using their car and he had an emergency so needed to quickly attend to it and he needed to drive there. He picked up my car around noon.'

'Did he say what the emergency was?'

'Something to do with one of his sons. I didn't ask any questions, just loaned him my car.'

'What time did he return the car to you?'

'I'm not exactly sure,' Nigel said. 'Sometime after 10 o'clock that night — I had already gone to bed. I had told Michael to just put the car keys through my letter box after he had parked the car if it was late when he got back.'

'Okay,' said Hackett. 'But for what reason would Michael want to kill Detective Wiley?'

'I have absolutely no idea,' Nigel replied. 'You'd have to ask him that. Maybe he and Chloe knew something else. It's nothing to do with me.'

Hackett and Smith explained that they would need to keep Nigel in the station under police custody. He was still a suspect in an attempted murder. And what they didn't say to him is that he was now also a prime suspect in the murder of Chloe Little. Everything he was saying was too convenient. Nigel seemed outraged.

'Don't you understand?' he said with his voice raised. 'I've given you everything you need. I've just *laid the pieces* down in front of you. Do I need to *put them together* for you as well? I mean, check my car. Michael's fingerprints will be all over it! Check the time stamps on my online posts from last night. I was clearly at home minding my own business.'

'Mr. Quail, we will certainly check out everything that you've said to us. You don't need to worry about that.'

Hackett and Smith excused themselves from the interview room and joined Hana and Luke on the other side of the glass.

'What the hell do you think about this?' Smith asked.

Hana shook her head and Luke looked at Nigel Quail, who had stood up and was now pacing back and forth behind his chair.

'Is this the guy who attacked you?' Hana asked.

'It's possible,' Luke said. 'Do we know for certain that Michael McPherson and Chloe Little were having an affair?'

'Nothing concrete popped up in our searches or interviews,' Hackett said. 'But that doesn't mean it's not true. We can ask around.'

All of the sudden, Nigel was next to the glass, rapping on it with his knuckles.

'Jesus,' Hackett said. 'Just a second.'

Hackett let himself back into the interview room and asked Nigel what he wanted.

'There's one more thing,' Nigel said.

Hackett moved towards the table and went to press the button on the digital recorder.

'Oh you don't need that,' Nigel said. 'I don't want to speak to you. I want to speak to Detective Wiley.'

Smith, Hana and Luke looked at each other.

'What do you think?' Smith asked them.

Luke considered his options for a moment and asked Hana for her opinion.

'Let's take a look at this guy's home first.'

'Agreed,' said Luke. 'And you'd better pick up Michael McPherson.'

Thirty-Two

Hana and Luke stood outside Nigel Quail's apartment building and watched the auto technicians affix clamps to the wheels of the white Ford hatchback and maneuver it onto the towing truck.

'We'll have basic prints and results from the first sweep through the car by tomorrow morning,' the technician said to the detectives.

Hana thanked him and they turned their attention to the building.

'It's a lovely block of apartments,' Hana said. 'They don't build them like this anymore. I think Hackett and Smith said that he's lived here for almost twenty years.'

'Your point being?'

'That he would have bought this for not much money twenty years ago. He works part-time at the local council. He's not making a fortune. He could do with that £50,000.'

'So,' Luke continued, 'this whole explanation of Michael concocting this swindle isn't entirely accurate.'

'Would you risk stealing £50,000 if you didn't have to? Would you just go along with someone else's scheme?'

'No. But the motivation of some people can surprise us. Let's go in, shall we?'

The detectives slipped on the protective shoe coverings offered to them by an officer at the front door and went inside. As Hackett and Smith had discovered before them, the apartment was tidy and a bit boring. The furniture would have felt comfortable in any basic rental accommodation, except Nigel would have chosen it all himself, and probably some time ago now.

In the sitting room, that morning's newspaper was open and folded neatly to the section he had been reading. A plate containing only crumbs from an eaten piece of toast sat on the table, an empty mug neatly next to it on a coaster.

'If you were going to design a completely uninteresting home, this would be it,' Hana said.

'I disagree, Hana. The most boring places tend to have the best secrets.'

'Oh great, we have Poirot with us this morning. Please, after you,' Hana gestured down the hall.

The IT team was in the study at the back of the apartment and looking at Nigel's computer.

'Obviously, we'll take it in for a proper look, but we've been briefed to scan for some time stamps and last internet searches first,' the IT officer said.

Luke nodded while Hana leaned over the desk, scanning it herself for any kind of answer. She asked the officer for a pair of latex gloves. Pulling them on, she picked up a pen sitting to the right of the computer and held it up in front of Luke.

Luke could see that it was a Montblanc fountain pen, not the kind of expensive implement that matched the rest of the apartment.

'Maybe he was a fountain pen aficionado? He might be that kind of guy,' said Luke.

Hana swivelled the pen so that the side of the pen was

facing Luke and she moved it closer to his face. There on the cap were small, monogrammed letters: CL.

'Where do you think he got this, then?' Hana said, placing it back onto the desk in the exact position she found it.

Luke didn't say anything. He knew that they were perhaps finally getting somewhere. What else was this home going to tell them? Nigel had been equal parts pompous and bewildered in the interview with Hackett and Smith. He appeared as someone who was used to getting his way but what did this mean in this particular situation?

The kitchen was as ordinary as the rest of the house. While Hana imagined that the rest of the apartments in the building would have a dishwasher, Nigel's did not and the dishes sitting clean and dry in the dish rack by the sink were all mismatched. She figured that he was the kind of person who lived alone, rarely had guests, and so used the same favoured plate and bowl and mug again and again. She opened one of the cupboard doors with her gloved hand and the dishes inside were also parts of different sets, like they had been procured from a charity shop, and stacked neatly in rows.

Hana and Luke were both instantly drawn to the one object in the apartment that betrayed the dullness of the rest of it. The refrigerator. It was covered in photographs — mostly printed on 6x4 inch glossy paper, a few cut very precisely from magazines and newsletters. They were arranged in a kind of collage but none of the photographs overlapped the others, like the rest of the house they were aligned neatly.

'What do you notice?' asked Luke.

Hana peered at the refrigerator doors and took her time in answering.

'Nigel Quail is in every single photograph.'

'Exactly,' Luke said. 'Fascinating that you would put all of these up, don't you think? Photos are mementos of those who are absent. That isn't what this is.'

Hana winced slightly to herself, her chest with a twinge of an involuntary ache. Luke had placed photos of Sadie in various spots in his house where he could see her when he was doing mundane things. There was a photograph of her on the shelf that sat to the right of his kitchen sink. Every time Luke washed his hands or filled the kettle, Sadie was there. Hana had noticed that a photo of Luke and Sadie that used to sit wedged between battered paperbacks on the bookshelf in their den had been moved to the mantlepiece next to the clock. Every turn of Luke's head to note the time and Sadie would be there.

But these pictures on Nigel Quail's refrigerator felt like a sort of mantra: *I am liked, I have friends, I am not alone.* They seemed to be a very personal confirmation that Nigel was part of the world around him.

Luke stepped out of the kitchen for a moment and returned as he slapped on a pair of latex gloves. He began to run his finger over the edges of the photographs until he came to the only one which didn't have a clear edge.

Luke pulled it off the fridge and it released easily, as if the sticky piece of tack on the back had recently been already disturbed. Hana looked over his shoulder at the thick paper, something that had been cut out of a brochure or magazine.

From right to left was Lucy, Venetia Wright, Nigel, and Chloe. Luke handed the picture to Hana and scanned the kitchen. He saw what he was looking for - the scissors sitting in the butcher's block on the counter.

Walking over to the counter, he stopped and looked around again before pulling open the drawer that sat directly in front of the knife set. Luke pulled something delicately out of the drawer and held it up in front of him. He turned to Hana and lowered the item to the left of the picture in her hand.

A thin three centimetre strip of paper was an exact match to the uneven edge of the photo in Hana's hand. And there on the missing strip was the smiling face of Michael McPherson, his outstretched arm brutally amputated, only his hand seemingly resting on the small of Chloe Little's back.

THIRTY-THREE

Lottie McPherson wondered if she had done the right thing. She also felt a bit queasy and she needed some air. Lottie poured herself a glass of water and opened the kitchen door to let the breeze filter through into the house. It was a chilly October day but she didn't care that the temperature inside was suddenly much lower, she needed to feel it.

Had she shown enough surprise that two detectives had shown up at the house? She hadn't wanted to let them inside — her instinct being to keep the conversation as short as possible, but the moment they asked her if she understood they had already come by three days earlier to speak to her husband, she knew she had to invite them in. It would have looked suspicious otherwise.

In the end, the detectives only stayed a couple of minutes. Did she know where her husband was? *Yes, I believe he's at the office.* Do you know where your husband was on Friday night? *He was out with work colleagues.* Do you know what time he got home? *No, I don't remember, but not too late as I was still up and watching tv on my laptop.* Do you own a car? *Yes.*

Where is it? *It's parked outside.* When was the last time either of you drove it? *A couple of days ago, I think.*

She had asked them what this was all about. When they didn't immediately answer, she asked if it was about Chloe Little. The taller detective had answered her with another question: had she known Chloe? Lottie answered this one as truthfully as she could. She said that she didn't really know her and had met her at Venetia Wright's funeral the year before. The committee was her husband's thing, not hers.

She had searched the detectives faces for what she really wanted to know, but didn't get a sense of it. Part of her had been relieved that they showed up at her door and she had been home to answer it. If truth be known, Lottie had wondered if she had been wandering around in a state of shock for the past few days after Chloe's murder had become public. But what made everything so much worse was the fact that her husband had said nothing about it to her. Why? She felt dread in the pit of her stomach when she thought about it and sipped from her glass of water.

They would have to discuss it eventually — the murder was now filtering out to become major news and it would soon be unavoidable. Now that the police had turned up at the door, she could bring it up without seeming odd. They needed to have a serious talk about Chloe Little and everything that had happened. She knew they both had secrets to reveal to each other, a final admission that neither of them would like. And above all, they had to get their stories straight.

What Lottie didn't know is that the two detectives hadn't really left. Hackett and Smith were sitting in their car across the street and a few houses down with an excellent view of Michael McPherson as he approached. It was the easiest arrest they had made in weeks.

THIRTY-FOUR

For a woman of Hana's height and slim build, Luke was always amazed at the amount of food she could eat. They sat opposite each other at the little bistro on the Strand, mostly filled with students from King's College London, at their usual table and Hana was devouring an entire half roast chicken and side of frites.

Luke pulled the slices of tomato out of his club sandwich with his one good hand and placed them on Hana's plate. Trying to eat a club sandwich with a broken collarbone and one arm in a sling had been a bad idea.

'Thanks,' she said.

The detectives ate in silence for another minute and Luke wondered if Hana was thinking that although it had been over a year since they'd last done this, it felt like no time at all had gone by. This is exactly what she was thinking, but not wanting to make a point about something that may not happen again if Luke slunk back into his early retirement, she focused on the case.

'So what's your takeaway from Nigel Quail's apartment?'

'Well,' Luke said as he wiped his fingers on his napkin,

'Looks like a weird guy. In love with Chloe Little. Not a lot else going on in his life. Obsessive? Killed her? It's possible.'

Hana's phone rang and she answered it with her mouth full, and then stopped eating. Luke knew there was something important being passed along. Hana was nodding and listening attentively and then hung up almost as quickly as she'd answered the call.

'Two things,' Hana said. 'One good and one irritating.'

'Go good first.'

'Hackett and Smith have picked up Michael McPherson. No issues there. They got him arriving home after speaking to the wife. She clearly didn't tip him off, so that's interesting.'

'And?'

'Forensics has come back on the anonymous note through your door. Nothing. It was clean.'

'It's not really surprising,' said Luke, shrugging his shoulders and biting into his club sandwich.

'Surely you have thoughts about where this note came from? I mean, you were attacked that same night.'

'Yes, that's the thing,' said Luke. Hana waited for him to finish chewing and continue his train of thought.

'It's precisely that these things happened on the same day that makes me think they're probably not related.'

'Come on, how can they not be?'

'I just don't think so. I think it's highly unlikely that I'm being warned off in both homes. Who would know both addresses? I'm guessing that the note is just a prank from whoever was using my office in Scotland Yard and would really like me not to take it back permanently.'

'Seriously, you think a cop did this?' asked Hana.

'The note? Yeah, could be. I'm not taking it all that seriously. I don't think there's anything to be worried about.'

'Look, I didn't really want to bring this up and float it as a possibility, but...do you think that Marcus Wright had anything to do with the note?'

Hana was surprised when Luke chortled at her suggestion. Having a sense of humour about anything to do with Marcus Wright wasn't something that Luke was usually able to do.

'What's so funny?' Hana asked. 'You think that I'm wildly off-base with that?'

'Probably. It's just...how do I put this? It's just that putting a threatening note through someone's front door isn't Marcus's style. He would think something so obvious was beneath him. A childish prank.'

'Do you know when you're going to speak to him?'

'A black eye and a broken collarbone doesn't exactly give the best impression,' Luke said.

'You don't have to do it, you know.'

'I do, Hana. Hackett and Smith got nowhere. He's only going to speak to me. We all know that.'

Hana put her knife and fork down and wiped her mouth with her napkin. She took a sip of water before she spoke.

'All I'm saying, Luke, is to be careful. Don't go looking for something that you aren't going to find.'

'Except I think that I am going to find what we need. Chloe Little went to speak to Marcus for a reason. That's the reason she was killed and probably the reason that I was attacked.'

'I'm not talking about Chloe Little and this case, Luke. You know that.'

'Hana,' said Luke, taking one last bite of his sandwich, the words muffled by a full mouth, 'what the hell *do* I know.'

———

Her Majesty's Prison Belmarsh in the dreary suburbs of southeast London is not somewhere you would ever wish to be. The brick blocks are constructed as the opposite of a labyrinth and the blocks are all adjoined at right angles. There is nowhere to hide. If a prisoner was able to escape from a guard, or shimmy out of a window, or miraculously hop a fence, they would find themselves trapped in a courtyard surrounded by other tall, imposing brick blocks. The mirror image of where they had escaped from. The entire prison is like a claustrophobic crossword puzzle.

Working in the Serious Crime Unit meant that Luke sometimes had to come to here to see a prisoner. They would never risk bringing Category A offenders out of Belmarsh. He hated it. Where some detectives would feel that they'd done their jobs well, had gotten the guy and now he was locked up — with a great sense of satisfaction — Luke felt differently. For him, Belmarsh represented the worst of humanity. It was maybe an odd sensation for a DCI to feel, but Luke was bothered that such depravity, such cruelty existed and here it all was right in front of him in one place.

When Luke entered through the security perimeter, flashing his identification and emptying his pockets to go through the scanner, he could feel his pulse quickening. He focused on his breath as he waited to be seen by the attending officer in charge, just as he would do in yoga class. He tried to centre himself.

The officer hung up his phone call and shook his head at Luke.

'Not visiting hours, I'm afraid.'

'I'll be on the list.'

The officer asked to see Luke's ID again and looked at the computer screen in front of him.

'Who are you here to see?' he asked.

'Marcus Wright.'

The officer's head snapped up and then he checked his screen again. He nodded at Luke.

'Follow me, Sir.'

Luke thought about what Hana had said at lunch. *Don't go looking for something that you're not going to find.* Was he looking for something? Was she right?

Ten minutes earlier, Luke had stood outside of the security perimeter at Belmarsh, staring at the imposing brick wall, wondering about the conversation ahead. Part of him was curious, and he hated that he felt this way. He wondered, too, what Sadie would think about it all if she was still here. He wished she was here. She probably wouldn't say anything to sway him one way or another, but he would know that he could talk to her about it.

Luke had pulled his phone out of his pocket and did something he'd never done before. He texted Nicky Bowman.

I'm just about to speak to Marcus Wright.

He had wanted her to know what he was doing. He had wanted to feel connected to somewhere safe. He cared very much what she thought.

Luke was still looking at his phone screen when the speech bubble popped up to show that Nicky was typing a response.

I'm here.

He knew that his phone would be taken from him as soon as he was escorted into the next block where the private visiting rooms were located and he tapped his fingers against the rectangular shape in his pocket as he followed the officer.

'My colleague has called ahead, so it will still be about ten minutes until we can book the prisoner all of the way to this block.'

'That's fine,' Luke replied, understanding that the physical book the guards still used would need to be signed at each stage of Marcus's brief journey from his cell to this interview room. It always took awhile.

Luke was shown into the interview room, the light from the slim windows faint at best, and he sat down on the chair facing the door. It was the only chair that moved, the other one bolted into the ground, a table similarly bolted into the stained concrete between them.

'I hope I'm not speaking out of turn, Sir,' the officer said.

'Yes?'

'It's just that Marcus Wright hadn't had a single visitor until two weeks ago. And now two in a row. And the other one...'

'Was murdered,' Luke said.

'Yes. I've only just seen that. Terrible. It's just, well, I suppose that's why you're here.'

'Did you attend to that visitation?' asked Luke.

'I did, Sir.'

'How long did they meet for? Was anyone else with Chloe Little?'

'She was alone, Sir. I'd have to check the logbook for the exact sign in and out times, but she stayed quite awhile. I'd say she was here for over an hour.'

'Okay, thank you officer.'

The door was shut and Luke was left alone to wait for the biggest mistake of his life.

Thirty-Five

Marcus and Venetia Wright left their house in Holland Park together. It was such a humid evening that stepping outside felt like a mistake, the sticky air and the hot, salty smell of London in summer clinging to them instantly.

Their taxi was waiting. Marcus had called it on his app and the driver later said that nothing was out of the ordinary.

Venetia was wearing jeans, ballet flats and a loose black blouse. Her keys and a credit card were slipped into her pocket. She had applied a deep wine coloured lipstick just before they left, standing in the front hallway and looking at herself in the oval mirror that hung on the wall by the front door. If she sipped her cocktails carefully, the colour stain would last throughout the entire evening.

'All ready,' Marcus said as he joined her at the front door, the small duffle bag in his hand.

'Do you want to take a jacket? It's always a little cooler up in Scotland.'

'Not a bad idea. One second.'

'I'll meet you in the cab.'

Venetia waved to the driver as she walked towards the car and hopped in. Marcus followed behind and Venetia could faintly hear the beeping of the alarm as he set it.

'I'll drop you at the bar and then continue onto the station, I have plenty of time.'

'No, don't worry. It's all a nightmare of a one way system there — it'll cost an extra ten pounds to get you out of there and then over to Euston. I'll hop out just past the hospital and walk in.'

'Are you sure? It's so hot out,' Marcus said.

'Darling, I'm fine.'

She squeezed his knee, the two of them sitting in the back of the taxi, windows open and the sounds of the hot summer night buzzing through the window as they made their way into the centre of town.

As they crossed over Tottenham Court Road, Venetia asked the driver to pull over. She told Marcus to have a good train ride and to call her in the morning. With a quick peck on his lips, she climbed over him to step out of the taxi on the pavement side. He smiled and waved his hand at her and the driver pulled back into traffic for the extra few blocks that would take him to Euston Station.

The driver told the police later that he had asked Marcus if he wished to be dropped on the street or if he should continue into the taxi rank so he was closer to the station entrance. Marcus had requested the latter and didn't seem to be in any rush.

It was just before 8pm when Marcus walked towards the ticket barriers at Euston Station. The Caledonian Sleeper always used the platform that sat farthest to the east of the station and seasoned travellers knew that you could go through the usual barriers, or approach the platform from further over next to the newsagent where passengers could easily walk through unobstructed. Marcus went to the barrier and held his phone screen that contained the QR code for his ticket over the scanner and waited for the barrier to open. He walked down the platform to the last car where first class and the club dining car were located. He stepped onto the train and found his compartment where he left his duffel bag, grabbed the key that sat next to his first class toiletry bag and complimentary water and locked the door behind him. Marcus made his way down the tight corridor to the dining car and walked up to the bar.

He greeted the barman and once again held his phone screen out for his code to be scanned. When Marcus asked to see a menu, the barman offered to seat him at one of the tables already laid with a crisp white tablecloth, cutlery and linen napkins arranged neatly at each place.

'Thank you,' Marcus said. He ordered the burrata salad and a glass of gavi, but hopped onto the barstool in front of him to sip his wine and chat until his food arrived.

The bartender later told the police that the conversation was completely unremarkable. They discussed the weather, train punctuality, the menu, the football results. Marcus stayed in the dining car for around an hour. He waited until the club car conductor walked through the dining car and stopped him to say hello. He had his QR code scanned one last time, checking him properly into his room and he told the conductor that he was going to turn in and try to get a good night's rest. He declined to have breakfast served to him in his room and the conductor marked this down on his tablet.

In his compartment, Marcus fought the urge to rush. He pulled back the covers and lay down in the bed, tossing and turning until the fitted sheet just came up on one corner of the mattress. He put one pillow aside, as if he didn't use it and made sure his head sank into the other one. As he sat up he noticed a couple of his hairs on his shirt collar. He carefully plucked them off his shirt and lay them on the pillow.

Marcus adjusted the window shade so that it was lifted up about three inches, which he would have done in the morning to let a bit of light in as the train coasted through the borders towards Glasgow. He turned the bedside light on and off, and flicked the switch to the power socket as if he had just removed his phone charger but forgot to switch it off again.

He picked up the bottle of water and emptied in down the sink before placing it in the garbage bin. Marcus opened the face wash from the toiletry kit and washed his face, dampening the towel a little bit more than necessary before roughly hanging it back up. He used the toilet and tore off the last few strips of toilet paper and flushed them.

Looking around the compartment for anything he may have missed, Marcus took a deep breath before opening the door a crack and looking out of the windows on the other side of the hallway that faced the platform. As he had hoped, the platform was now extremely crowded with hundreds of passengers walking down it and boarding his train. This was his moment. He picked up his duffle bag, pressed the 'Do Not Disturb' button on his door, turned off the light and exited quickly. Marcus joined the throng of passengers, ducking away from the train and weaving his way through the crowd of people pulling cases. The train on the other side of the platform was boarding as well as the crowd surged past him and Marcus veered away from the barriers towards the exit that he hadn't used earlier, into the newsagent and out the other side towards Euston Road.

He pulled a black baseball cap out of his duffel bag, tugging the zipper as he walked, and pulled it onto his head. The speed of pedestrians around Euston Station suited him and he walked briskly across the main road and into the little streets of Fitzrovia. The car was parked where he had left it and this had been a risk. It was unregistered with a false license plate and it had been parked there, unmoved for more than three weeks. He hadn't dared check it in that time and was relieved to see the windshield free from parking tickets. Here was London efficiency at its best, he thought, a sigh of relief that the car plates wouldn't have been checked by an officious parking monitor.

Marcus unlocked the car and put his duffel bag in the footwell. He unzipped it again and pulled out the small hunting knife. He carefully placed it inside his jacket pocket and locked the car. Within five minutes he was standing at the top of the cobblestone alley that led from the street towards the cocktail bar. Moving into the shadows a few houses down from the entrance, he pulled out his phone and looked at the time. It was coming up to ten o'clock. Marcus swiped the screen on his phone to pull up the real time departures board from Euston Station. His train had left on time and was already on the outskirts of London, making its way up the country towards the north.

He had thought the next move through at great length. He knew exactly what he was going to do.

Just minutes later with the timing he knew was perfect, Venetia walked out of the bar and turned left into the alleyway. It was dark, there was very little ambient light where Marcus was waiting for her and she only realized that it was him at the very last moment. It was better that way. Marcus didn't note any look of surprise or confusion or fear on his wife's face as he stabbed her twice. Quick, sharp movements.

He did not let her body drop to the ground. Marcus eased her towards the cobblestones, her head turned away from him. She did not struggle. He removed her watch and bracelet and didn't look back.

The knife was slipped back into his pocket and then he began to run. He ran a full two blocks before slowing down to normal speed and diverting up to the car once more. His jacket with the bloodied knife was placed inside a plastic grocery bag and stored in the trunk. Marcus started the car and pulled out of the spot where it had been parked for these last three weeks and began the crawl out of the city towards the motorway.

He realized that he was still panting, more from stress than from the run back to the car, and he pressed the button to open the car window, the hot summer air finally feeling cool to his skin as it flooded into the car with the wind of the car's movement.

Marcus had taken a life and seemingly shattered his own. It was easy to not think about what had just happened, what he had just done, because he wanted to focus entirely on his driving. It was a long seven hours ahead of him and one error — a speeding ticket, a wrong turn — could snare him. Eyes were on the road in front of him, water was in the cup holder next to him, and his phone was turned off.

Seven hours and twelve minutes later, Marcus was parking on a quiet residential street about fifteen blocks away from Glasgow Central Station. It had taken months of searching on his business trips to the city to find this road where he figured that this unregistered car would not be searched or noticed for months. When it was finally moved, it would simply be sold on, all evidence of his crime already removed and who would be looking for it anyway?

This is what he thought to himself as he casually strolled over towards the station. He kept his head down just in case, but any CCTV camera that did pick him up would be irrelevant. No one would ever think to look for a man that was on a train that hadn't yet reached the city.

This was the one factor he couldn't control — the time of the train's arrival. He couldn't turn on his phone to check the train's progress or the exact arrival time and he couldn't enter the station from the front to look at the arrivals board. He would have to hope that it came in relatively on time.

Marcus waited down the street from the station, watching the inbound trains crawl into Glasgow Terminus and about five minutes ahead of schedule came the distinctive turquoise carriages of the Caledonian Sleeper. He quickly darted back towards the side entrance of the station and waited. He had changed his jacket in the car and felt in the right hand pocket to check that his phone was there and then joined the crowd of passengers who had just stepped off the sleeper. Marcus was as bleary eyed as the rest of them after driving non-stop for over seven hours and he stifled an honest yawn.

He didn't move quickly and he resisted the urge to look around him. He waited until he could see the main CCTV cameras pointing towards the trains from the front of the station's inner hall and slowed down as he removed his phone from his pocket and pressed the button on its side to turn it on.

The messages popped up again and again and again, all overlapping each other so that his screen was filled with dozens of notification bubbles. He slowed down and looked at the phone, willing it to ring.

It rang.

As he slid his thumb over the screen to answer, he looked up at the CCTV camera and cleared his throat.

THIRTY-SIX

L uke wasn't sure what he was expecting. A year in Her Majesty's Prison Belmarsh and Marcus Wright looked well. He was slightly slimmer, pale from lack of sunlight, but he looked rested and like he was arriving to meet an old friend for a drink and a catch up — in prison scrubs.

'Luke,' said Marcus, 'how lovely to see you. Been in a bit of a tussle, I see. That eye needs some ice.'

There was no reply from the other side of the table.

'I'd shake your hand, but,' Marcus lifted his hands as much as he could until the chains of the cuffs jangled and became taught. He was double shackled with his hands together in one set of cuffs and a second set of cuffs bound his hands to the table leg in front of him.

'Before I ask to what I owe this generous visit, can I ask how you are doing?' Marcus leaned forwarded and lowered his voice. 'How are you getting on without your lovely wife?'

Luke had been prepared for this. He knew this was something that Marcus would say, although perhaps he didn't imagine that he would lead with it. Again, Luke did not reply. Marcus Wright was a talker and the best way to get what he needed out of him was to let him do just that. Luke ignored the deep urge he felt to punch the guy's lights out.

'Did they ever find out what actually happened? I mean, what caused Sadie to veer off the road like that?'

They hadn't, in fact, been able to determine why Sadie's car ended up in the lake just off the A119. The most logical explanation was that she swerved suddenly to avoid an animal. Sometimes Luke found himself wondering what animal it may have been — a deer? A rabbit? At that time of the early evening, it could even have been a badger. He had been angry at Sadie in these moments, wishing she had just hit it. Damage to the car, a dead animal, but he would still have his wife.

Luke shrugged his shoulders and exhaled. Marcus kept going.

'And why couldn't she get out of the car before it went under the water? Did they ever determine that?'

Luke hoped that his flinch wasn't visible to Marcus. He bit the inside of his cheek just slightly to pull himself out of what he was thinking.

'How have *you* been Marcus?' Luke finally said. 'Belmarsh seems to suit you.'

'Well, it's not The Robson, but I make do.'

Perfect, Luke thought. He wants to get right into it, so we will get right into it.

'You told Chloe Little that she may be able to find me at The Robson.'

'I did, yes. Did she?'

The answer to this exact question is one that he had thought about for the past couple of days, ever since they realized that Chloe Little had been to visit Marcus in prison. Does he obfuscate here and not let on that Chloe was killed before she could find Luke? Or does he come clean and see what follows?

Just as Luke explained to Hana that arranging for an

anonymous note to be put through his front door wasn't
Marcus's style, Luke knew that if he had a sense of power over
the detective, Luke might get more out of him. He might just
get the answer they needed to crack this.

'I'm afraid not,' Luke said. 'She was killed first.'

'I'm sorry to hear that.'

'Why did she come to see you?'

Luke always asked the question that would get to the question you really wanted to ask. And he knew that Marcus
would want to talk, so Luke let him.

Chloe Little turning up to speak to Marcus had been a
complete surprise. He couldn't remember ever meeting her
previously during the committee days when they all worked
for Venetia, but he supposed that he must have done so at
some point. He had pretended that he did remember her.

She had been very upset, quite tearful and wanted to talk
about Venetia.

'I thought this was a little strange, don't you agree?'
Marcus said. 'Why would you come to talk about Venetia with
the man who killed her?'

Chloe had been trying to relieve her guilt. She told Marcus
about the money, how they had stolen it and no one had yet
noticed as everything was still being dealt with in a long
probate after her death, now that Marcus was behind bars.
Who better to confess to, to try to assuage her guilt, than to
the man who should feel guiltiest of all? That is what Marcus
had thought, but that wasn't really the reason for her visit.
Not the main reason, anyway.

'Which was?' Luke asked.

'To ask me about you,' Marcus replied.

'I will confess that I'm not following, Marcus. I had never
met Chloe Little before — it was my partner who did her
interview when Venetia died. What did she want to know
about me? And why?'

Marcus leaned forward in his chair so he could reach his face with his elbow at the only angle where he could scratch his face while cuffed. He leaned back and smiled.

'Precisely,' he said. 'I couldn't figure it out either. She kept asking if you were trustworthy, if you were really not working for the Met anymore after you, well, you know.'

'And what did you tell her?'

'I told her that I liked you enormously. You were, in fact, one of the best people I had ever met. Completely trustworthy. That the death of your wife meant that you were suddenly a very wealthy man and I doubted you would return to work. So I must say, I'm rather surprised to see you here.'

'And you gave her my address in the Cotswolds.'

Suddenly Marcus looked puzzled. A flash of irritation crossed his face, as if he had just lost the upper hand in this conversation.

'How did you know that?' Marcus asked.

'And you told her that if I was in London, I would be at The Robson on a Thursday night.'

'Well,' Marcus said. 'That had been my suggestion after all. After Sadie died, I said that having a ritual each week of going somewhere you loved together would be an enormous comfort.'

Luke said nothing. He hated that this was true.

'Are you not going then? So Chloe couldn't find you. She couldn't tell you the secret she was desperate to confess.'

'But she told you.'

Marcus smiled.

'It's so good of you to come, Luke. I have missed you.'

Luke could feel what he needed slipping away from him. He was being outplayed yet again. It had been a mistake to come here. Hana had been right.

'You and I are the same, Luke. We have both known a

great love. We have both been deeply loved by an incredible partner.'

The maelstrom of emotion that swirled in Luke as these words came out of Marcus's mouth were overwhelming. How dare he compare the two of them? How could he understand great love? It was impossible.

'I can see what you're thinking,' Marcus continued. 'You are thinking: how dare he talk about this. He killed his wife.'

'Something like that,' said Luke.

'But that's not what I mean. Listen to what I am saying. We have known the love of a wonderful woman. We have felt loved. Imagine if you hadn't. Imagine if you were desperate for it. Imagine if you had spent your whole life desiring it, it finally came to you and you discovered that you were wrong.'

Luke wondered what this had to do with anything, but knew that Marcus Wright never uttered a single word that didn't mean something. He listened carefully.

'You know what I can't bear, Luke? Killing someone out of greed is one thing. Abhorrent, yes. Here I am.' The chains on his cuffs clinked together as Marcus pointed to himself.

'But killing someone out of fear is quite another thing,' he said. 'It is cowardly. Chloe Little did not deserve such an ending.'

'Who killed her, Marcus And why?'

'I don't know. But I'll tell you something: the proof is always recorded. The record is with someone who remains. My home wasn't where Chloe died, but the origins of her death lie there.'

Luke knew better than to ask any more questions of this man he despised. All he was going to get was another riddle. Marcus was clearly enjoying himself. Luke wanted to get out of there — he'd had enough.

As he stood up to leave and banged on the door to alert

the officer so he could exit the suffocating room, he couldn't resist it. He had to ask Marcus one more question.

'Marcus, you don't actually have a brother, do you?'

Marcus Wright looked at Luke and smiled.

'Only child, I'm afraid.'

———

When he arrived home, Luke noticed the envelope right away. It was bigger than the other envelope but the same white paper and like the first one, it was unsealed. Luke looked at it lying on his doormat for a moment, debating whether or not to find a pair of latex gloves somewhere in his house and put them on before picking up the envelope.

But this was all surely a prank and after his afternoon at Belmarsh, he was irritated. Luke picked it up and pulled out the contents of the envelope. This time it wasn't a piece of paper, it was an 8 x 10 photograph.

Luke held it in between his fingers, his brain struggling to keep up with his emotions. He couldn't breathe. He couldn't believe what he was seeing. No. No, no no. He forced himself to take a breath in the moment that his entire life changed again.

THIRTY-SEVEN

Hana was sitting at her desk on the seventh floor, looking through CCTV of Nigel Quail's car where it was picked up in a couple of places around Bluffs Cottage. The footage was grainy and the driver couldn't be clearly identified.

'DS Sawatsky, good afternoon.'

Hana looked up to see Marina Scott-Carson standing in front of her. She noticed that the floor was quieter than usual, the sudden hush a symptom of this unusual appearance from the Commissioner.

Hana stood to attention.

'Ma'am, good afternoon.'

Scott-Carson smiled and pointed to Luke's empty office.

'A quick word, detective?'

Hana and Scott-Carson moved into the space next door and closed the door behind them. Neither woman sat down.

'So how is he doing?'

'Wiley is doing well, Ma'am.'

'How does it feel to have him back?'

Hana hadn't been expecting this question. She hesitated.

'I'm not sure what you mean. I'd always prefer to work with DCI Wiley. We were a great team. But I don't believe he is back. I mean, it was good of you to reinstate him for this case. I feel we're getting there with it.'

'And then?'

'Ma'am, I'm sorry. I'm not following.'

'You have a lot of sway with DCI Wiley, Sawatsky. I may be sending O'Donnell to an early grave, but should Wiley wish to return full-time, I would encourage that if I were you.'

Hana nodded and thanked her. Scott-Carson didn't need to say anything further. Her point had been made and she glided down the hallway back towards the lift in her navy heels and matching wool cape. The dress code got more elaborate the higher up you got in the building and Hana was relieved to work on the seventh floor, still comfortable and casual.

When she returned to her desk, Smith was waiting for her.

'We've got Michael McPherson in interview room three. Why don't you come in with us?'

'With pleasure,' Hana said.

———

Michael McPherson's demeanour was the opposite to that of Nigel Quail when the detectives were questioning him. He was extremely nervous and looked occasionally to be on the verge of tears.

To be honest, Hana didn't particularly remember him from the Venetia Wright case when she interviewed the entire committee. She found it hard to believe that all of the committee members were back in this criminal context. They had seemed to her such an uninteresting group of people at the time. Clearly, Hana had misjudged them.

Michael McPherson insisted that he was working on

Friday evening. Unhelpfully, he said that he had been working from the pub.

'You were working from the pub. On a Friday evening.' Hackett sounded a little more than sceptical.

Michael explained that it was boring work — looking through old reports and filing them — nothing that took any real brain power and he liked a quiet pub around the corner from his house and to nurse a pint while he did it.

Hana stood behind Hackett and Smith in the interview room and stared at Michael. Was this the guy? She always was able to trust her gut instinct and it was usually right. She had been right about Marcus Wright. It had caused such friction in her relationship with Luke. But she had been right.

Did Michael McPherson kill Chloe? Her gut was telling her nothing.

It was as if Michael knew that he was backed into a corner and had to begin talking. And it began to sound familiar.

'Look, I know I am here about Detective Wiley being attacked.'

All three detectives in the room were suddenly paying attention. None of them spoke.

'It was Nigel Quail.'

Hana stepped forward.

'How do you know that?'

'He told me that he was going to do it. He said he was going to kill him. I didn't believe him, but he called me this morning and told me what had happened.'

'And what did he say had happened?'

Michael shifted uncomfortably in his seat. Hana couldn't tell if he was stalling for time to make something up, or if he didn't know how much he should reveal.

'I had called him on Friday morning. Just to check in. It's been such a shock with Chloe's death. He seemed totally crazy on the phone. He said that Chloe had told Detective Wiley about something he had done. I didn't know what he was talking about. Nigel seemed to have lost it. I went over there and he said he was going to drive out to the Cotswolds to speak to the detective and he asked me to come with him.'

Hana felt like they were finally getting somewhere. One of the three of them on the committee was going to break and maybe this was it.

'What had Nigel done?'

Michael shrugged his shoulders and shook his head.

'I honestly don't know. But Chloe knew. I...I think that Nigel might have killed Chloe.'

'Why would Chloe know what Nigel had done, but you did not?' Hana asked.

'Nigel was a little bit in love with Chloe. We all knew it. I guess he wanted to confide in her.'

'Weren't you a little bit in love with Chloe Little?'

As soon as these words were out of Hana's mouth, Michael began to cry. He was fighting it, but the tears came anyway and he cleared his throat, wiping the tears away with the back of his hand.

'I was very fond of Chloe,' Michael said.

'Were the two of you having an affair?'

Michael bowed his head and the word he uttered was barely audible.

'I'm sorry, what was that?' Hana asked.

'Yes.'

'Did the others know?'

'Yes. I mean, I didn't think so but we all met for coffee the other day and they told me that they knew.'

'Did your wife know?'

Michael's head snapped up as soon as Hana asked the question. He looked panicked.

'No. No, she doesn't know. Oh god, please. This has absolutely nothing to do with her.'

Hana's phone began to vibrate in her pocket. She pulled it out and saw Luke's name on the screen. She pressed the side button to silence the phone and slipped it back in her pocket. Luke had more patience that she did and Hana knew that he wouldn't call again, understanding that if she wasn't picking up, it meant she was likely driving or in the middle of something important. He would send a text next letting her know what he wanted.

Hackett knew that now was the time to press the suspect in front of them. He turned to look at Hana and she understood.

'Can you tell us again where you were the night that Chloe was killed?' Hackett asked.

Michael shook his head and closed his eyes.

'I had nothing to do with Chloe's death. I didn't do this.'

He's lying, Hana thought.

'Where were you, Michael?'

'I've already gone through all of this with you. I was asked out to drinks with my work colleagues that night. Then I had one other pint at another pub on my way home and looked at my reports.'

Hackett looked like he was disappointed in Michael. He liked to do this in an interview as the suspect always gave something away when confronted with a facial expression that had a hint of sympathy while simultaneously letting them know that they were already one step ahead.

'The thing is, Michael. We've checked out your story already and your colleagues confirmed that you left around 8:30pm.'

'You've spoken to my colleagues?'

'Is that really the first thing you have to say after we've told you that you have no alibi for the evening that Chloe was killed?'

'But,' said Michael. 'I do. I do have an alibi. I went to The

Three Horseshoes just off Albion Place. You can ask in there. I was in there all night. Then I just went home.'

'You seem to spend a lot of time in pubs, Michael.'

'Please you have to believe me. Nigel killed Chloe. He's done something else too, but I don't know what. I went to his house on Friday after I called him and he sounded crazy. I agreed to drive with him to the Cotswolds and speak to Detective Wiley. We had an argument in the car before we had even left London, so I got out and went home. The night that Chloe was killed I was with my colleagues and then in The Three Horseshoes. That's it.'

There was tapping on the glass wall behind them. Hana poked her head outside and Rowdy was standing there. She let herself out of the interview room and shut the door behind her.

'Sorry to interrupt,' Rowdy said. 'But thought you would want to know. I have both Michael McPherson and Nigel Quail's phones here with me. They keep ringing. It's the same person calling both of them. And she keeps calling.'

'Let me guess,' said Hana. 'Lucy Bishop.'

'The one and only.'

'Thanks, Rowdy.'

Hackett and Smith joined Hana outside the interview room. Michael had been asking if he could leave.

'I told him that he'd be here a little bit longer. And that Fraud may want to have a quick word.'

Hana left them to it and pulled out her phone. Luke's text startled her. There were only two words on the screen:

Please come.

THIRTY-EIGHT

Lucy didn't know what to make of neither Michael nor Nigel answering their phones but she had a pretty good guess. They had both called her that morning, ranting about the other one. Nigel was the more hysterical of the two, but Lucy would have expected that. He insisted that Michael was trying to frame him for Chloe's murder. Lucy, not normally one to want to engage with Nigel beyond what was strictly necessary, kept him on the line and asked him to explain what had happened. She had tried not to panic as he rambled on about the events of the previous day. This is how she learnt that Michael had called him and asked to borrow his car. When Michael arrived to pick it up, he urged Nigel to come with him to speak to Detective Wiley.

'He was so arrogant, Lucy. He wanted to put me in my place by telling me that he knew where Detective Wiley lived in the Cotswolds, as if his relationship with Chloe was more meaningful. Chloe had already asked *me* to come with her to the Cotswolds, I knew where the detective was already!' Nigel seethed.

Nigel had refused, saying he was not going to get any

further involved in their giant mess — one that was Michael's doing in the first place.

'I waited for him to bring the car back. He didn't return until after midnight. I confronted him about what had happened but he just brushed me off and refused to speak to me. I couldn't believe it.'

'But why did you loan your car to him then in the first place?' Lucy had asked.

Nigel didn't answer.

So Lucy wasn't surprised to hear from Michael that morning. He had rang and said he was coming over to speak to her.

'I'm busy, Michael.'

'I'm almost there, Lucy,' he replied and Michael had pleaded with her to see him. He sounded desperate and that made her nervous. Would one of these men break, the way that Chloe did? Would one of them go to the police and ruin everything?

Lucy couldn't help but feel a little thrill when Michael told her his side of the story. Nigel had rung him the previous morning and asked him to come to the Cotswolds to speak to Detective Wiley. They needed to find out what he knew, didn't they? Had Chloe spoken to him before she died? This set off alarm bells for Michael. Had Nigel been the one? Did he kill Chloe?

When Michael arrived at Nigel's apartment, Nigel had insisted that they get on the road and they could talk in the car. So Michael got in and off they went. Except that they argued about the approach they were going to take with Detective Wiley and Michael had asked Nigel to pull over so he could get out. The last Michael saw of Nigel, he was speeding away in his car towards the M4 motorway.

They had turned on each other. Lucy guessed that they were being questioned again after one of them confronted Detective Wiley. Whichever one did it.

Idiots.

She couldn't care less which one of them was being accused of Chloe's murder. What concerned her was Lottie. She knew that she had to take care of it.

Nigel being arrested was one thing. He was a spare part. He was irrelevant to their futures. But Michael wasn't. He had invested Venetia's money, and to her knowledge no one had missed it yet, and Michael needed to be here to finish off what they had started.

Nigel and Chloe had been adamant about not continuing on with their plan after Venetia's death. But Lucy absolutely wanted that money. Michael had remained neutral on the subject, refusing to be drawn into a decision one way or another. That had been a good sign. But if Michael was arrested now, everything would fall apart. Did Lottie know about the money? Could Lottie continue with the investment if something happened? Lucy doubted it. She doubted it very much.

———

After trying both Michael and Nigel's phones for half an hour, Lucy knew what she had to do. She grabbed her jacket and her bag. She would make her way to Michael and Lottie's house. Something made her stop briefly and she turned around to check that what she had taken was exactly where she had hidden it. This object was her lifeline. She cursed herself for this paranoid behaviour, like checking to see if you'd locked your front door only seconds after you'd locked it.

Lottie didn't seem particularly surprised to see her when she opened the door. The two women stared at each other for a second before Lottie said, 'My boys are inside.'

'Well,' replied Lucy, 'Shall we go somewhere to talk? I know what you did.'

THIRTY-NINE

A huge range of emotion bubbled in Hana as she sped towards Luke's house.

Please come.

Whatever it was, it was serious. She had tried calling but there had been no answer. Instead, three more words flashed up on her screen from Luke.

Please just come.

Had Luke been attacked again? Hopefully the fact that he could text meant that he wasn't hurt. But something was really wrong. Why would he need her there in person?

She was desperately worried, but at the same time a hint of relief washed over her. She felt grateful. She was grateful that their relationship had repaired itself enough to have this level of need and this amount of trust.

Things between them hadn't been going well just before Sadie died. The Venetia Wright case had everyone on edge and

Hana was beginning to doubt her partner. It was a horrendous feeling — one that she kept trying to shake off, but it stuck to her like a burr. She couldn't easily pick it off.

None of this was helped by the atmosphere in the Serious Crime Unit. Word had spread that Luke was spending an unusual amount of time with Marcus Wright and while it made Hana uneasy, it was beginning to anger her colleagues. Luke and Marcus hanging out didn't sit well with anyone, despite the fact that Marcus's wife had been murdered.

And that was the thing — Hana had felt that they needed to dive deeper into Marcus Wright as a suspect. They had no one else — half a dozen men had been arrested and released without charge. They were beginning to look very foolish. Marcus had been ruled out so quickly because of his alibi — he couldn't possibly be sleeping on a train hundreds of miles from London at the same time Venetia was stabbed to death. But for Hana, this didn't mean that he wasn't involved some-how, and the fact that Luke wasn't also thinking this, meant that he was too close to Marcus. He was too close emotionally to the whole situation and Hana told him as much.

It didn't go down well.

They had argued, loudly and at length, and Hana couldn't remember this ever happening before. In that moment, their relationship began to splinter and once that happened, she knew it would be extremely tough to repair it. Partners who were successful in their jobs trusted each other entirely — their opinions even when differing had to be respected. Hana had been devastated, but also had to admit to herself that she and Luke weren't doing a good job on this case. She constantly thought of Venetia, how her black blouse stuck to her not from the heat of that humid July night, but because it was soaked in blood.

Hana had begun to investigate Marcus Wright again, on her own, and she told no one. She was barely speaking to

Luke. And then the phone call came in that changed all of their lives. In one moment, everything they knew was shattered, their universes suddenly spinning on a different axis and their lives were altered forever.

Hana and Luke had clung to each other in this new, foreign universe, a universe without Sadie, but the argument about Marcus Wright was not forgotten. And shortly after Sadie's death, it would be blown wide open again.

FORTY

When Hana arrived at Luke's house, she rang the bell. There was no answer. The panic began to rise in her throat as she pictured Luke injured on the other side of the door. She grasped the door handle and tried it. The door swung open and Hana darted inside, calling for him.

'Here.'

The voice came from the kitchen and Hana ran towards it.

Hana stopped short. She had seen him like this once before. Standing there in Luke and Sadie's kitchen, seeing Luke sitting on the floor, his back against the kitchen island felt like a recurring dream. Hana felt that time had shifted and it took her a moment to focus.

'Are you alright?'

Luke shook his head.

'Are you injured? What has happened?'

Luke shook his head again and Hana crouched down to sit next to him.

'Jesus Christ, Hana.'

He was whispering.

Hana felt fear radiate throughout her entire body before she even knew what she was supposed to be frightened of. She tried to form words but found that she couldn't, and that's when she saw it on the floor beside him.

It wasn't just one photograph, it was three of them. Hana looked at them, one by one. Her hands began to shake.

Jesus Christ.

Three photographs blown up to 8x10 inch prints, as if to make sure that Luke understood what he was seeing.

It was Sadie. She was in the driver's seat of her car. Whoever took the photograph was sitting in the backseat diagonally to her. His gloved hand was holding the back of her seat. But what stood out immediately were Sadie's hands — her knuckles were a shocking shade of white as she gripped the steering wheel.

The second photograph made Hana gasp. It was the same, except the camera was pointed at Sadie face on. She looked terrified.

The final photograph was the most chilling thing Hana had ever seen in all her years of police work. It was Sadie's car mostly submerged in the lake, but taken close up. The photographer would have been standing right next to it in the shallows of the water.

'Hana,' Luke whispered again.

Hana could only nod, and she grabbed his forearm and gripped it as tightly as she could.

FORTY-ONE

I t's funny how you can react well in the moment, but fall apart afterwards and that is what happened to Chloe. She hadn't been blindsided when Michael ended their relationship. She could tell he had been pulling away from her. All of their conversations about the future and what they would do and where they would travel and how their life would be had stopped.

Michael had come over to her house after work, which gave them the usual two or three hours before any excuse of staying late at the office would no longer hold up and he had to return home to Lottie. They hadn't bothered to eat. As soon as Chloe poured the first glass of wine, Michael began his little speech. That's what it sounded like: a little, prepared speech.

Chloe couldn't quite take in what Michael was saying, as she grappled with why he was speaking like this to her. It was Michael. They didn't ever have awkward conversations or were formal. They were a unit. They were a couple.

At first, Chloe thought he was speaking in this rehearsed manner because he was trying to hold it together for himself.

He must be devastated to be doing this, he is trying not to cry, she thought.

All Chloe could muster was a bewildered, 'I don't understand.'

Michael was quiet when she spoke and answered softly.

'I know you don't understand, Chloe. I am so sorry. But I have to give my marriage a chance. I owe it to Lottie, the boys, and to what we have built together over all of these years. I just have to try.'

Chloe tried to talk to him, not to reason, or to plead with him not to leave her, but to get him to say more. Anything else at all. But Michael had nothing else to say, except *I have to try.*

Chloe didn't want to hear it, so she told Michael to leave. When he was gone, Chloe was surprised at how calm she felt. It was a bump in the road and really, she should have been expecting this. Of course there was going to be a moment of hesitation, a moment where the guilt became too much for Michael. It was incredible that this moment had taken so long to arrive. It was nothing that they wouldn't get through together. Chloe would give Michael a day or two to sit with his feelings, a day or two to begin to miss her and then she would speak to him again.

The third day after he said it was over, Chloe called him. She called his burner phone, the one she always called. He had bought it soon after their affair began, and she hadn't thought anything of it at the time. She had been too excited about this man and how instantly they had connected. But as it rang and rang and Michael wasn't picking up, Chloe began to feel angry. It was a rising tide of anger and she felt hot and gripped the phone tightly in her hand. When there was no answer, she called again and began to pace her living room, the anger turning to a blind panic when he didn't answer.

Had he meant it? Had Michael actually left her?

The tears began to come then as the heat in her body

rushed out of her in huge, gulping sobs. She began to shake and curled up in a ball on her sofa. *Oh my god, oh my god*, she thought. He had really left her. She couldn't bear it. She couldn't go on.

Chloe lay in the fetal position on her blue, velvet sofa. The sofa she had picked out for the life she dreamed she would have. The sofa Michael sat on, so nervously that first evening he came over, and all of those evenings since, when the dream became the reality she had imagined. She blinked through her tears that blurred the faces in the photographs on her fireplace mantel as she watched her future fall away from her.

Except she had a trump card. She had the one thing that all of them didn't know she had.

———

Chloe figured that she had one last move. She would move her last piece into position — checkmate — and whichever way it happened, she no longer cared. It was all or nothing and she would play it that way. But she needed some advice first.

Shouldn't all four of them have been thinking about Venetia Wright? She seemed to be the only one of the committee who felt guilt about what they had done. This plan that Michael concocted to invest her money and then split the proceeds. Think of it as a loan, he had said. How shocking that they all went along with it. How terrible Chloe felt at the role she had played. And then Venetia was murdered.

It had all been so dreadful. Michael and Nigel seemed unaffected, but it was Lucy's lack of sympathy that had shocked her the most. Had Lucy forgotten about their time in India with Venetia? How the three of them had bonded, how they had talked late into the night, how they had shared the kind of private details of their lives in a way you would only do when taken completely out of your usual environment?

Chloe had not forgotten any of it. She had not forgotten how impressive Venetia was, how kind and welcoming she was to them. She felt ill when she thought about how they had effectively stolen from her and even worse when she thought about how Venetia had died. What had come over her that she was able to betray Venetia like this? She hoped that Venetia would understand, that she would have given Chloe and Michael her blessing if she had known about their relationship before she died.

Michael, Nigel, Lucy and Chloe had not spoken much about the murder investigation. It had happened so soon after Michael had siphoned off the funds that they were all nervous they would be found out. But Chloe had followed the case in the media — it had become an absolute circus. All of these men arrested and then released. Marcus finally being charged with his wife's murder. The lead detective leaving the Met. She had read every article, taken everything in. And now she knew that she needed to speak to Marcus Wright.

Only hours after the unanswered calls to Michael's burner phone she had requested the appointment. She couldn't believe how easy it was to figure out how to put in a visitor request for an inmate at Belmarsh Prison. It had somehow made her feel braver. She thought about all of the people who made appointments to see their loved ones in this prison every week. *How amazing that we are surrounded by criminals and don't even know it*, she thought. When it came down to it, she was a criminal as well, so she would do what she needed to do.

———

When Chloe returned from seeing Marcus Wright, she needed to call Michael one more time. She had guessed that he wouldn't pick up, but she still felt the disappointment like an ache in her jaw. She grit her teeth together and sent a text.

I've been to see Marcus Wright.

Her phone screen lit up the next morning around 7:30am and it was the usual burner phone number. She answered the call.

Michael voice was cold and seething.

'It is over, Chloe. Do not ever call me again. I am getting rid of this phone. I don't care if you need to deal with your own guilt by talking to Marcus. But don't be foolish.'

'Michael, are you sure you don't want to talk this through? I understand how difficult this is for you. Let's just talk.'

There was a brief pause on the line, as if Michael wasn't sure how to respond. Chloe had told herself that she would give him one more chance. One more shot to realize for himself that what he was choosing was the wrong choice.

'It's over, Chloe.'

He didn't take the shot.

'I'm sorry that you feel this way Michael. But you are about to be extremely sorry.'

'Come again?' Michael asked.

'Do you think your actions don't have consequences?'

And then Chloe told Michael exactly what she was going to do.

FORTY-TWO

Chloe Little was forcing herself to have conviction about what she was going to do. She sat in the lobby bar at The Robson and looked around her, scanning for any sign of Detective Luke Wiley. The brief thought crossed her mind that Marcus Wright was having her on — maybe the detective had never set foot in this hotel and sending her here for no reason is what Marcus Wright did for fun. She resisted the urge to pull the piece of paper with Luke Wiley's image on it from the pocket of her coat which rested on the back of her chair. She had printed the photograph out from her Google Image search and stuck it to her pinboard at home. Every time Chloe walked by the printed photograph she told herself that she was going to do it. She thought about what Marcus Wright had told her about the detective. How he had walked away from it all. Luke Wiley's face became a sort of talisman for her — she, too, would walk away from that old life. She would burn it to the ground.

Chloe sipped her gin and tonic, the ice now mostly melted in her tumbler. She checked behind her to confirm that there wasn't another entrance to the bar and then kept her eyes peeled for the detective. As every minute passed she felt more and more nervous, and she had been so preoccupied with the decision to seek Detective Wiley out that she hadn't rehearsed what she was going to say.

Should she stand up and ask him to join her and then explain why? How would he react? She would have to confess how she knew he was going to be in the lobby bar at The Robson and how would that play out? Marcus Wright had given her two locations where she would be sure to find the detective, the details of which she had shared with Michael and Nigel. She would have preferred to have this conversation privately but Michael had flatly refused to have anything to do with her and scoffed at the idea of driving to the detective's home in the Cotswolds. Michael had come close to threatening her if she went through with her plan but she didn't care.

She had tried one more person — sweet but sad Nigel Quail. She had asked him in person, over drinks, hoping that she could get him on side one more time. He had refused as well.

Men — they were always incredibly disappointing.

As Chloe watched the ice melt in her glass, she felt her confidence in her plan dissolve along with it. She looked up at the bar entrance one last time and then signalled to the waiter for the bill.

The former Detective Chief Inspector Luke Wiley had stayed at home on this particular Thursday evening, neither of them knowing how this decision would affect both their lives.

———

Chloe had dragged herself into the office the next day and it was midday when a text message pinged onto her phone.

When she saw the name that lit up in the text notification, her heart leapt into her throat.

It was Michael. It was Michael texting from his actual phone, the phone he hadn't used to communicate with her in over a year.

Had her threat worked? Chloe's hands were shaking as she picked up the phone and slid her thumb across the screen to reveal the message's content.

I've been thinking about you. Missing you. Can we meet? Don't call - please just text ASAP.

He wanted to meet. He was texting from his actual phone. The relief that flooded her body made her skin tingle. She felt tearful, so happy that her fears were being wiped away, that the future she imagined was still right in front of her and she was going to be able to grasp it. She didn't think about her response in any great detail before she typed it.

Of course. Mine? Anytime works.

The reply text came back almost instantly.

I had somewhere else in mind. London St. James Hotel? I'll text you the room number later.

Chloe stared at the screen. She was absolutely thrilled. The rest of the day passed in a blur. It felt like she was encased in a haze of happiness and any thoughts she had about what she had planned to do now felt foolish. She had a twinge of panic about what Marcus Wright knew. Would he tell anyone? Would he use this knowledge as leverage somehow? Chloe doubted it. The guy was in prison with a life sentence and it was his word against hers. The only piece of evidence was upstairs in her bedside table. It was sitting there, completely innocuous, no one knew she had it except for Marcus Wright. She could always get rid of it later if she was really worried.

But for now Chloe had to figure out what to wear. Why was she so nervous? This is what she had wanted for over a year and it was finally happening. She pulled out dress after dress and tried them on, discarding them on her bed when one of them didn't seem right. Maybe dress trousers and a shirt with heels? Michael had always found that very sexy. Outfits were pulled on and taken off until she finally decided. The chaos of her room was unlike her, and as she turned to look at the mess before switching off the bedroom light, she smiled. She was finally walking into her new life.

The text that told her to come straight to room 412 popped up onto her phone as she was making her way to the hotel. It was a warm evening for October and she was a little early in her eagerness to see Michael, so she hopped off the bus in Knightsbridge and decided to walk the rest of the way through Green Park towards the hotel.

As she walked through the park, she pushed all previous thoughts aside — she could have blown this entire new life apart before it had even begun — and she smiled at the version of her future that was now in front of her.

As she walked through the lobby of St James Hotel and made her way towards the lift, she couldn't help but think about this particular framing of events. Last night, The Robson Hotel where she almost made a terrible mistake. Tonight, a different hotel and the love of her life waiting for her upstairs. After all this time it was to be their official beginning.

The elevator whisked Chloe up four floors and she walked down the long, dimly lit corridor towards room 412 which was the last room on the right. She knocked softly on the door and waited for it to open. Chloe smiled in anticipation and then bit her lower lip out of excitement, a habit that Michael always said he loved.

The door swung open and all of the air in Chloe's body seemed to rush out of her lungs as if she had just landed from a height. She tried to take in a breath and couldn't and the face staring back at her smiled.

FORTY-THREE

The tragedy of Sadie's death had been the greatest shock of Luke's life. It had seemed impossible to compound the tragedy further or to make his grief more acute. But as Luke and Hana held the photographs of the moments before and after Sadie's death, they both realized that what had seemed impossible was fully, unimaginably possible.

There had only been a few moments of silence when Hana reached Luke, sitting on the floor of his kitchen, and saw the photographs herself. It was Luke who spoke first.

'She was killed, Hana.'

Hana could only nod as she pulled herself up from the floor and walked over to the large table by the window that overlooked their garden and sat down again.

'I don't understand,' Hana said. 'Who would want to kill Sadie?'

Luke was wide-eyed and kept shaking his head. Hana stood up again and poured two glasses of cold water from the kitchen tap. She handed one to Luke and sipped from her own glass.

Luke held the glass of water in both hands and then turned to look at Hana. She knew he had just made a decision.

'Do you think you know who did this?' Hana asked.

'No,' Luke replied as he finally peeled himself off the floor and came to sit with Hana at the table. 'But, Hana, we will tell no one.'

'You can't be serious, Luke.'

'I'm absolutely serious. We tell no one. It could be anyone — think of how many people we have put behind bars. Think about the note through my door and now these photographs. Who has my address? I'm not that easy to find. They must have had help.'

Hana couldn't believe what she was hearing, but she also knew that Luke was right.

'You think this possibly has Met involvement?'

'I'm not sure,' Luke said. 'But I'm coming back to work and we are going to find out who killed my wife. And why.'

Hana tried to swallow the lump in her throat. It was what she had longed to hear Luke say for over a year, but the circumstances that prompted him to say it were devastating.

'I've got you,' Hana said.

Luke reached over and squeezed her arm.

'I know.'

It was at this point where in their old life, food would be ordered because Hana would be starving and Luke would happily eat whatever was put in front of him. The two detectives would eat and talk and figure out the case. But neither of them were hungry and couldn't imagine being so for quite some time. They did, however, begin to talk it all through. They did not talk about Sadie and her death. It seemed impossible. They knew that they simply could not do it. Instead, they talked about the other case in front of them, the one that Luke knew would bring him at least one desperately needed answer.

'I saw Marcus Wright.'

Hana nodded.

'Annoyingly, he seemed well.'

'Are you okay?'

Luke was the one who nodded this time.

'Yeah, I'm fine. Maybe I needed to see him one last time. And he definitely knows something. Chloe Little had been to see him as we suspected. He said something quite specific to me.'

'What?' Hana asked.

'Oh you know Marcus. It was a goddamn riddle.'

'You're kidding.'

'No. He said it very clearly.'

'Okay, go on then,' said Hana. 'Try me.'

Luke hesitated for a moment before repeating the words Marcus Wright had uttered in the bowels of Belmarsh Prison. He had thought of nothing else as he drove home from the prison, knowing that these three sentences held the information they needed to understand what exactly Chloe Little wanted to tell Luke. Marcus liked to play a game, but he knew when he had already been beaten. The riddle would be stacked with clues. All Luke and Hana had to do was figure them out.

'Bear with me, Hana. You know how this guy operated. He said — *The proof is always recorded. The record is with someone who remains.* And then he said — *my home wasn't where Chloe died, but the origins of her death lie there.*'

'What the hell, Luke. Did he say anything else about Chloe's visit?'

'Not really,' Luke said. 'Only that she was distraught, and he asked me to imagine what it would have been like to feel unloved.'

'What the hell does that mean?'

Luke took a deep breath. 'It was weird, Hana. It was as if he was trying to comfort me in my own loss somehow. Like he was saying: Sadie may be gone but she deeply loved you and you know how that felt. He was inferring that Chloe had never felt this kind of love. It made her do something.'

'Something that got her killed.'

'Yes, I believe so.'

'Did you ask Marcus if she was having an affair with Michael McPherson?'

'No. As usual, I didn't ask him much at all. He just talked.'

Hana looked down at her hands. This was Luke's way of apologizing. She knew he was sorry for all of the holes in the Venetia Wright murder investigation that he refused to talk through. She knew that his mistake had torn him apart. It was enough. He didn't need to be sorry anymore.

'Hana, you saw what I didn't last time. You took another look at Marcus. You felt that he was the killer. What made you look?'

They had never really talked about it. Sadie's death had interrupted any recriminations between the two detectives.

'I don't like things that don't make sense, Luke. It didn't make sense that Marcus was latching onto you while he was grieving. I thought at first that I was jealous, but it wasn't that. Something was just off to me.'

'I would normally have felt that, too.'

'Yes, you would have. But nothing felt normal about the Venetia Wright case.'

So Hana had looked again. She went back to the members' only cocktail bar and found the last date that Venetia had been there. It had been three weeks before her murder and when Hana dug into the passenger records of the Caledonian Express for this exact same date, she found the name she was looking for on the manifest — Marcus Wright. But on this evening the train had been delayed by over two hours and then eventually cancelled. It was here that Laura Rowdy worked her magic. They had picked Marcus Wright up on CCTV leaving

Euston Station after the train had been cancelled. He did not go in the direction of his home in Holland Park.

Instead, they followed him all the way to a side street four blocks away from the cocktail bar. Door to door canvassing found two houses with their own door camera surveillance and one of these caught Marcus Wright next to a car. The license plate was unregistered.

It took another two days of going back over Automatic Number Plate Registration for the evening that Venetia Wright was murdered. Hana vividly remembers the look on Laura Rowdy's face when she turned up at the station that morning just over a year ago. It was a look that said: *We got him.*

And they had. At a petrol station just outside of Carlisle, cameras picked up the unregistered license plate pulling up next to the petrol pump and Marcus Wright getting out of his car to fill it up. It turned out to be incredibly easy to be fast asleep on the Caledonian Express, chugging your way up to Glasgow at the exact same time you were filling your car with petrol on the Scottish border.

It had only taken another two hours to locate the car, still parked on an unassuming side street in Glasgow, a dozen penalty fines attached to the windscreen, Venetia Wright's blood on the steering wheel, the front seat and in the truck of the car.

And now the Chloe Little case felt eerily similar.

'Let's look at Chloe Little again,' Luke said.

'Okay. Well, assuming she was having an affair with Michael McPherson, I would look at him first. How often is it the person closest to the victim? Pretty often.'

'I think she had proof, Hana. I think that's what Marcus meant by 'the proof is always recorded'. It's a photograph, or a video or something that provides proof for something else.'

'What is the something else?'

'Exactly. I don't know. But if the proof is with one who remains, that probably isn't Chloe. It's one of the other committee members.'

'Okay,' said Hana. 'But this is needle in a haystack stuff, Luke. How can we be looking for proof of something when we don't know what the something is?'

'Because Marcus gave us one more clue. The origins of her death lie in Marcus and Venetia's house,' said Luke.

'But we know that already. We know that Marcus came up with his plan to murder Venetia when they lived in that house and we know that Chloe and Venetia were connected from the committee meetings that took place in that house. Those are the two deaths.'

'Yes,' said Luke. 'Unless there is another death.'

FORTY-FOUR

Lottie had led Lucy through the house and across the small garden towards Michael's office shed. The two women stood across from each other and Lottie reached around Lucy to shut the door behind them.

'Two detectives have taken Michael to the station for questioning.'

Lucy didn't say anything and waited for Lottie to continue.

'My husband did not kill Chloe Little.'

'No?' Lucy replied.

'It's thanks to you that we are in this mess in the first place, Lucy. This fucking committee of yours. What the hell do you want?'

'This is *my* fault?' Lucy asked, incredulously.

Lottie was angry. She slammed her fist into the shed wall and it made Lucy jump. But it also gave her an entrance. If Lottie was this angry, there was a good chance she would be able to give Lucy what she wanted.

'How long have you known about their affair?'

Lottie didn't say anything, weighing up what answer she was willing to give.

'I know what you did, Lottie.'

There was a very long pause as the two women sized each other up.

'I don't know what you're talking about.'

'Really?' Lucy asked, incredulously. 'You just asked me to come out here so your kids don't hear us. I think you absolutely know what I'm talking about. You killed Chloe.'

Lottie looked like she had been punched.

'I did not kill Chloe,' Lottie hissed. 'You're crazy.'

'She called me, Lottie. She told me what you did.'

———

Lucy had come close to not picking up the call at all. When she saw Chloe's name on her screen, she felt a surge of anger. She knew that Chloe would be calling to moan about Michael. She would go on and on about the relationship; she would talk endlessly about her despair that he had ended it. Lucy couldn't bear it anymore. Chloe's reaction had gone from tiresome to unseemly and honestly, what did she expect was going to happen? This is how their last conversation had ended. Lucy had been particularly unkind and she knew it.

'Chloe,' she had said. 'Did you really think Michael was going to give up his entire life for you? It just wasn't going to happen. Why would he do that?'

Chloe had sat in stunned silence on the other end of the line. A few curt words were exchanged and they hadn't spoken since.

The only reason Lucy picked up the phone was because she wondered if Chloe had information about the money. She needed this investment to pan out and maybe Michael had said something. She could not have been more wrong.

Chloe was hysterical.

The whole story came tumbling out of Chloe through giant, heaving sobs. Michael had texted her. He had been desperate to see her and booked a hotel room for them. She was convinced he had left his wife.

When she got to the hotel room, it was Lottie who opened the door.

'She knew all about the affair, Lucy. She knew about what happened at Venetia's house that night. She knew fucking everything. She threatened to go to the police if I didn't leave Michael alone.'

Lucy had lazily answered the phone on speaker, but after hearing this she turned off the speaker and gripped the phone tightly to her ear.

'What do you mean she knew about what happened at Venetia's house that night?'

'Michael must have told her. She has known all along.'

'How did she threaten you? What exactly did she say?' Lucy asked, the blood beginning to pump audibly in her ears as the panic began to rise in her chest.

'She fucking knows everything, Lucy. She said she would blame me for what happened if I didn't stay away from Michael.'

'She has no proof, Chloe. Right? She doesn't really know what happened.'

It was at this point Lucy's blood ran cold. Chloe had stopped crying and sounded very alert, very clear and utterly chilling.

'Exactly,' Chloe said. 'But I have proof. I still have the phone that he recorded everything with. I have it. And I'm going to the police first. I will show Michael that he made a mistake. A huge fucking mistake.'

'But that's not possible,' Lucy stuttered into the phone. 'We got rid of the phone.'

Chloe began to laugh and said she had to go.

The line went dead and Lucy stared at the phone in disbelief. Then she grabbed her shoes and her jacket and walked out the front door.

————

Now as she stood in the garden shed, Lucy thought that she held all the cards. But she wanted to understand exactly what Lottie knew in order to play them in the right order.

'I know you booked a hotel room and confronted Chloe,' Lucy said. 'She called me afterwards and told me everything. Within an hour of that phone call, she was dead. Did you kill her yourself, or did Michael help you?'

'Look Lucy, don't be ridiculous — of course I didn't kill her. Nor did Michael.'

'Well, he's currently with the police being questioned isn't he? So maybe we'll see about that.'

Lottie began to cry very quietly and Lucy saw her opening.

'Do you know about the investment with Venetia's money?'

Lottie nodded.

'Can you access it? Or do you need Michael for that?'

'I'm not sure. I probably can, it's in a joint account but I don't know what I would do with it. I'm not a banker.'

Lottie may have threatened Chloe, but it was an empty threat. It was the threat of a tired, unappreciated wife. It wasn't desperate or calculating. It wasn't anywhere near what came out of Lucy's mouth next.

Lucy couched her threat in the guise of a bargain. If Lottie and Michael moved the money into the investment as they had all planned, and then paid Lucy her share — or all of it if they didn't want to be involved anymore, she didn't really care —

she would tell the police it was Nigel. He could finally be useful.

'But did Nigel kill Chloe?' Lottie asked, wide-eyed.

'Who cares, Lottie. He certainly attacked the detective, and if we go to the police and tell them that he confessed to us, what are they going to believe?'

'I don't know, Lucy. I'm not sure I'm comfortable with this.'

Lucy had been expecting this answer. She had been expecting this mousy woman who had been walked all over by her husband for the past year to not want to commit to her plan.

'The thing is, Lottie, you may know what happened in Venetia's house that night and you thought you could threaten Chloe with that information. But you have no actual proof. I have it. So what would you like to do?'

FORTY-FIVE

Hana Sawatsky may not have remembered Chloe Little and the other three committee members when it emerged she had interviewed them just over a year earlier, but they certainly remembered her.

Chloe, Lucy, Michael and Nigel had all been summoned for questioning at police headquarters the same afternoon. Ordinarily, this would seem like a unique experience in their lives — not exactly something one does every day — and they all wanted to be able to help the police catch Venetia's killer. Except nothing about it was ordinary and all four of them had not slept a wink. The previous evening had shaped the rest of their lives.

Venetia had been found murdered in the alley by the cock-tail bar just one week earlier and yet the committee members, in the way one often functions after a tragedy, decided to keep their meeting date as scheduled. They usually met at the Wright residence and Marcus insisted they do so as usual. He let the four of them in before excusing himself and headed out for the rest of the evening. Marcus liked his routine and despite losing his wife, he still went on his long evening walks to clear his head and get some exercise.

But about five minutes after Marcus had left, the doorbell rang. Every single of one them wished later that they hadn't answered the door.

At the door was a young man who introduced himself as David Ryan and he walked into the house without being invited inside. He seemed to know the house already and headed straight for the grand living room where they had assembled for the meeting. David Ryan introduced himself as a new employee of Venetia's holding company and he was still trying to get a handle on all various aspects of her work, including her charity endeavours. Venetia had planned to introduce him to everyone at this meeting, but after her death he had decided to come on his own.

The four committee members had looked at each other nervously, but said nothing. What David Ryan had actually interrupted was a massive argument. What were they to do now with the money that had been taken from Venetia and about to be invested? They couldn't possibly give it back without it being noticed now and they felt guilty to continue with the scheme when Venetia had just been murdered. Or at least some of them felt guilty.

Accusations were flying around the room and Chloe had just pointed out that they could all be considered suspects after this theft. All of them were slightly anxious about the police interview the next morning.

And that's when the doorbell rang.

As David Ryan sat down, the four of them attempted to talk about the charity. Chloe launched into an explanation of upcoming fundraising events and Lucy detailed the education plans for the schools in Goa. Michael and Nigel were largely silent, smiling and nodding along.

David Ryan took everything in and then suddenly stood up. He walked over to the fireplace and crossed his arms.

'Thank you for the overview,' he said. 'Very helpful. But perhaps you can guess that there is a specific reason for my visit today.'

All four of them felt their stomachs sink and no one said a word, waiting for one of the others to speak.

'We know about your theft of Venetia Wright's funds. She came to me last month to discuss her suspicions. Would anyone care to explain?'

As the one who always tried to take over a conversation, the one to insert himself where he never really belonged, Nigel tried to explain. He bluffed and he blustered and clearly had no understanding of anything financial as he attempted to refute this man's accusation.

It was Michael who finally told Nigel to shut up and then told David Ryan that the funds were moved from Venetia's account with her knowledge and approval and once the investment had matured, the funds would be returned with their interest to further support the charity.

'I'm afraid that Venetia did not approve this investment. You know this and I know this.'

'Well,' replied Michael. 'It's a very sad situation, but now that Venetia is gone there is no way to verify it.'

'Except there is.'

'I'm sorry?' Michael said.

David Ryan moved towards the bookshelf to his left and reached behind a box of long stemmed matches, removing a mobile phone and holding it up so that everyone could see it.

'Everything you have said tonight is being recorded. Venetia was terribly upset that you had stolen from her when she trusted you all implicitly. She did not want to confront you herself until she had proof. I am going to guess that your conversation before my arrival will provide that.'

The four of them stared at the phone screen in horror, the digital second hand ticking forward as David held the phone aloft. It had been recording for over an hour. They all knew that every single one of them was now caught red handed.

A flash of anger surged through Michael as he felt exactly how he always felt at work. Demeaned, not taken seriously, and mocked. He stood up to face this young guy who had just appeared out of nowhere to ruin their lives. Arrogant and patronizing just like the traders at work. David Ryan looked like he couldn't have been more than twenty five years old. How dare he turn up here and accuse them? Who the hell did he think he was?

'Look here, this is absolutely ridiculous. You can't record us without our permission. This is outrageous.'

Michael wasn't finished there, he began to shout at David and eventually Nigel stood up to try to calm him down.

'Oh will you get off me, Nigel. Back off!'

'There is no need to get so upset,' said David and when Michael heard these words, he snapped. He turned to this obnoxious young man who should never have been here in the first place and shoved him.

David Ryan slammed backwards into the fireplace mantle, the intricate wooden carving so loved by Venetia and shipped back from India winding him badly. He reached up to the mantle with his right hand, desperate to hold onto something as he tried to take in a breath and his knuckles caught the leopard vase, knocking it over. The sound of the vase smashing into hundreds of pieces shocked them into silence.

'Jesus, Michael,' said Chloe as he stood up to see if David was alright.

'I'm sorry,' Michael muttered.

But as David Ryan regained his composure, he looked wild-eyed and angry. He waved his phone in front of Michael's face and spit was flying out of his mouth as he shouted that he would put them all in jail.

Michael began to panic and looked over at Nigel for some sort of support.

'Can we just talk about this?' ventured Nigel, but David was rushing towards the back door and scrambled to find the latch to unlock the entrance to the upper terrace.

'What are you doing?'

David Ryan got the door open and stepped outside, Michael and Nigel following him.

'Don't touch me,' hissed David. 'I'm leaving.'

He looked down at his phone and stepped backwards.

'Watch where you're...'

It was too late. David Ryan misjudged his footing and stepped backwards one more time. The nineteenth century house did not have railings on the upper terrace, only a low wrought iron balustrade. Michael and Nigel watched in horror as he dropped from their view. They all heard the crack of his skull on the flagstone terrace below them.

FORTY-SIX

L uke had called Rowdy while he and Hana drove back to the station and he had asked for two things. He wanted the date of the last committee meeting that had taken place in Venetia and Marcus's house, which could be pulled from the Venetia Wright case file. And he needed a complete list of any suspicious deaths or homicides from that date and the following week.

Rowdy knew better to ask why these two things were being requested and got to it. She also relayed one other piece of news.

'They've released Michael McPherson from custody,' he told Hana.

'What? Why?'

'He's been cleared. We have CCTV footage of Nigel Quail in a petrol station just off the M40 on the night I was attacked.'

'Well, that wasn't very clever,' said Lucy.

Luke chuckled.

'Not particularly. Hard to believe this is the guy who broke my collarbone, but there you are.'

'But Hackett and Smith didn't want to hold McPherson for Chloe's murder?'

'Cleared with that, too. He was with his work colleagues and then seen in the same neighbourhood at a pub on his own. He was nowhere near Parsons Green on the night Chloe was killed. Fraud has made an appointment with him to go through any irregularities in Venetia Wright's finances and will determine what he was involved with, but in terms of Chloe Little, he didn't kill her.'

'Did Rowdy sound pleased on the phone? She loves the evidence piling up one way or another.'

'Let's see what she pulls up for us when we get there. But then, yes, we probably owe her a drink.'

Hana wondered what Luke was thinking as their car sped towards the Embankment. She knew that his brain had switched to laser focus mode because he felt he was close to cracking this case. She loved it when he was like this and she pushed aside the maelstrom of emotion that was swirling inside her after seeing the photographs of Sadie just moments before her death. She would find whoever did this. For now, she was going to help Luke find the killer of Chloe Little.

They swiped their passes at the entrance to Scotland Yard and headed upstairs. Rowdy had been looking toward the elevator door every time it opened, and when she saw it was finally Luke and Hana she waved them over.

Luke couldn't help but smile. Rowdy had found something which meant he had been right.

'Okay, ready?' Rowdy asked.

Luke and Hana nodded at her.

'The last committee meeting according to the interviews of all four members of the committee that were done by Hana was the evening of July 19th. I pulled up all suspicious, unexplained or homicides for that day and the following ten days.

There were only ten deaths to look at, but one popped right out.'

'Stop teasing me, Rowdy,' said Luke.

Rowdy looked like a proud mother and turned her computer screen to face the detectives.

'This one. David Ryan. Originally classified as an unexplained death, later changed to suicide. He died from blunt force trauma from a fall and was found by dog walkers at the bottom of the Hampstead viaduct.'

'And this one popped out, why?' asked Hana.

'David Ryan worked for Beckers, the accountancy firm. Beckers was the firm that Venetia Wright employed.'

'I don't understand,' said Hana. 'His death didn't come up when we were investigating Venetia's murder in the first place?'

'No,' Rowdy replied. 'He was just an employee there, very junior. I think he had just started at the firm. We didn't have him as specifically working for Venetia — as far as we were concerned, they had never met.'

'Interesting. Well, let's take a look, shall we? Well done, Rowdy.'

Luke sat down at Rowdy's desk and began to click through the electronic files of the case. When he got to Dr. Chung's medical examiner report, he stopped scrolling and read the report in detail.

'What is it?'

'Here,' Luke said, pointing at the screen. 'Chung writes that there are contusions on the back that aren't consistent with a fall. That he had to have been in some sort of other accident possibly prior to his death. Are there postmortem photos we can see?'

'Sure,' said Rowdy. 'Just here — you need to click this button.'

Luke followed Rowdy's instructions and a series of photographs of David Ryan's body appeared on the screen. Some were of the body at the location he was found and the rest would have been taken by Dr. Chung during her examination.

Luke clicked through the photographs and stopped cold when he got to the one of David Ryan's back and torso.

Luke's intake of breath was audible and both Rowdy and Hana looked at him.

'Can you please print this one, Rowdy?'

'Of course.'

Hana asked Luke what he saw, but he simply raised his hand as if to ask her to wait and when Rowdy brought back the piece of paper with the bruised back of David Ryan on it, he picked up the nearest pen on Rowdy's desk.

Luke traced the outline of the dark purple bruise, suddenly eliminating the gaps in the image. The resulting picture couldn't have been clearer — the bruise was in the perfect shape of an elephant's head, it's trunk and tusks marked indelibly into David Ryan's flesh. Only someone who knew the inside of Marcus and Venetia's house intimately would have seen this creature jumping out from the splotchy trauma of the bruise.

'The origins of death lie here.'

'Oh my god. He was killed in Marcus and Venetia's house,' said Hana.

'And Marcus knew it.'

'The proof is always recorded. The record is with one who remains.'

While Rowdy looked bewildered, she knew enough to keep quiet as the detectives figured out whatever they saw in front of them.

'Rowdy, if you were going to record a crime, how would you do it?'

'With a phone. Either video or audio. It's small and it's easy.'

Luke and Hana knew they were so close. But who had the proof and what would it reveal?

A voice called out from outside Rowdy's office.

'Is DCI Wiley in there?'

Luke stood up and stepped out into the hallway. One of the junior staffers was holding a phone receiver against his chest.

'Yes?'

'A call for you, sir. He says it's urgent.'

'Who is it?'

'He says his name is Michael McPherson.'

Luke rushed down the hall to the officer and grabbed the phone out of his hand. Rowdy and Hana watched Luke and waited for him to say something.

After a moment or two, Luke finally spoke.

'We'll be right there. Stay where you are.'

He passed the phone back to the officer and instructed him to get Hackett and Smith.

'Tell them to call me. Sawatsky and I are en route. Thanks, Rowdy,' Luke said, as he rushed down towards the elevator and Hana grabbed her jacket to follow him.

'What is it?'

'Michael McPherson said that when he got home his wife was missing. He thinks she is with Lucy Bishop.'

'Why does he think his wife is missing?'

'I'll explain on the way. We're about to find out who has the most to lose.'

FORTY-SEVEN

C hloe had been the one who picked up the dead man's phone. It had landed on the terrace next to him when he fell and was still recording. A chill went through her when she pressed the stop recording button.

None of them checked for a pulse. It was Marcus who did this when he returned home about an hour later. The four of them knew that Marcus had to be in on David Ryan's deception. How else would he have been able to plant his phone in the bookshelf? But the gravity of the situation wiped everything away and Marcus took over the moment he realized what had happened. The four committee members were all in shock and they had been grateful that Marcus was so calm. He told them what to do and they followed his instructions, so thankful that he seemed to know exactly how to handle the situation. It was only much later that the four of them understood why this happened, that Marcus couldn't afford another suspicious death on his doorstep.

They waited until dark and then moved the body into Michael's car. He and Marcus drove to the deserted bridge over Hampstead viaduct and dropped the body of David Ryan over it. Marcus had asked what happened to David's phone and Michael lied. He told Marcus that they had already gotten rid of it. It was only half a lie — Chloe had volunteered to do this after the body was disposed. She had held the phone in front of the dead man's face to unlock it and they had all listened to the recording of their argument. It could not have sounded worse.

But Chloe did not dispose of the phone on the way home. Something made her hold onto it. No one knew this until the night she was killed and she told Michael, Nigel and Lucy in turn that she had kept the phone with its incriminating recording and was going to reveal everything to Detective Chief Inspector Luke Wiley.

But only one person knew that she was physically carrying it with her the night she was tricked into meeting Lottie at the St James Hotel.

———

Luke and Hana were speeding towards Lucy Bishop's flat in Earls Court.

'Michael got home after being cleared by Hackett and Smith when the CCTV footage came in and his two boys were home alone. They said that their mother left the house quickly with another woman and that their mother said they had to tell their father this as soon as he got home.'

'At least we think we know what we're looking for when we get there,' Hana said.

The officer support that they had requested was already outside Lucy Bishop's building and standing unseen to anyone inside, as Luke had instructed.

Hana rang the buzzer for Flat 1 and they waited. When Lucy answered the door, officers immediately moved in and pulled Lucy to one side, pinning her arms behind her back and handcuffing her. The flat was small and Luke and Hana heard a voice call out from the kitchen. It was Lottie.

'It's here. I have it.'

Lottie was holding a mobile phone in her hand and Luke could see that it was turned on. He took the phone from her and the screen wallpaper showed a young man with his arms wrapped around a pretty girl. It was David Ryan.

'I have it, Hana.'

But Hana didn't reply. She was already in Lucy's bedroom, pulling on a pair of latex gloves as she yanked open the wardrobe in the corner. She quickly moved each hanger along the rail and examined every article of clothing hanging there but couldn't see it. A flash of blue caught her attention from behind the door she had just walked through. She closed the bedroom door so she was now alone in the bedroom, sealed away from the noise of the officers who were informing Lucy Bishop of her right to a solicitor. The bathrobe hanging from the singular hook on the back of the bedroom door was navy blue and well worn. She gently pulled it towards her. The belt loops were empty. Even though the bathrobe belt would likely never be found, Hana knew that the blue fibres from the robe would match the ones found on Chloe Little's neck.

They had her.

FORTY-EIGHT

D r. Nicky Robson couldn't help but be a little worried. She couldn't call Luke, or text him, to check in as she felt that would be overstepping her professional boundary. But Nicky found herself checking her email and her phone in between sessions with her other patients to see if there was any message from him.

There had been five days between their scheduled appointments and as Nicky waited for Luke to arrive, she found herself making a pot of espresso on top of her stove. She pulled out two espresso cups and slowly swirled the coffee in the pot before pouring out the steaming brew.

'Thank you,' Luke said as he accepted her offer of a pick me up when he arrived and Nicky carried it upstairs for him as his arm would be in a sling for a couple of weeks yet.

They sat down across from each other and Luke sipped from his cup.

'This is very good,' he said.

'Good.'

Luke didn't know where to begin and he told Nicky this.

'How are you feeling after seeing Marcus Wright?'

'I'm okay. It wasn't the most pleasant of experiences but bizarrely, he did help with this case. We've arrested the person who killed Chloe Little.'

'Congratulations,' said Nicky. 'Is that an appropriate thing to say? I've never congratulated a detective on apprehending a murderer before.'

Luke laughed out loud. Nicky smiled at him as this was the first time she'd ever seen him do it.

'Well, you may be saying it again,' Luke said. 'I've made the decision to go back to work.'

'Oh my god, that's quite big news.'

Luke knew that it was. He also knew that for now, he couldn't tell his therapist the real reason he was returning to the Metropolitan Police Force. Part of him couldn't bear the thought of having to describe what the photographs of Sadie in the car just minutes before she was murdered looked like and another part of him didn't want to bring Nicky into this story yet. He needed to be sure of what the story looked like first.

They talked about this transition back into his old life throughout the session and when the fifty minutes were up, Luke stood up to leave.

'Oh there's one more thing,' he said.

'What's that?'

'I had to talk to my boss about the parameters of my returning to work.'

Marina Scott-Carson had been receptive to his request, but she had been strict about three conditions. The first, that he remain partnered with DS Hana Sawatsky.

The second, that he still report directly to Chief Inspector Stephen O'Donnell.

'The third is that I undergo regular counselling with a therapist. I told them I had that covered.'

Nicky smiled at her patient, intrigued by what would be coming into their sessions together.

'You got it.'

———

Hana was waiting for Luke outside and as it was Thursday night, she suggested the one thing she knew Luke would be up for.

When they arrived at The Robson, Luke was escorted directly to his usual table.

'You weren't with us last week, Mr. Wiley,' said the host. 'Have you been up to anything interesting?'

'Oh you have no idea.'

The host simply smiled and confirmed that Luke would like his usual drink of choice. As they waited for their cocktails to arrive, Hana asked Luke what he wanted to do about the photographs.

'Honestly, Hana? I don't really know. But there was no reason to harm Sadie unless she was a threat.'

'What do you think that means?'

Luke waited for the waiter to place his vodka gimlet in front of him. Hana picked up her gin and tonic and sipped it.

'I think Sadie knew something and it got her killed.'

'What on earth could she have known that you and I did not?'

Luke picked up his gimlet and for the first time in over a year felt clearheaded and calm. He was grateful for Hana's loyalty to him and her perseverance with how difficult he must have been over the past several months. He thought about Sadie and the very first time she brought him to this hotel and he felt the love that he had for her surge even more strongly through him on this evening all of these years later.

'I don't know. But we are about to find out.'

IF YOU ENJOYED A GRAVE RETURN...

Please consider leaving a rating or a review on Amazon, it really helps new readers discover DCI Luke Wiley and the team.

DCI Luke Wiley returns in

The Quiet and the Dead

Read on for the first chapter...

PROLOGUE

After what she had been through over the past six years, the paranoia was always there. She woke every morning in her quiet room and on sunny days the light streamed through the window, the shadows from the tree branches outside dancing on the bedroom walls. She never slept with her curtains drawn, so desperate she still was to feel the light and the air and the outside world around her.

She had created a safe space for herself but she knew she was never safe. She knew they were still out there watching her.

Her three flatmates didn't know anything about her past. They thought they did — she had made up a boring one. She said she had parents and a sister and they lived up north. One weekend when her flatmates were all away, she took the opportunity to lie and say that she was also away, visiting her family. Instead, she stayed in the flat, enjoying the peace and quiet and above all, she enjoyed the space. She couldn't have visited her family anyway, even though she was desperate to see them.

She knew that she could not be complacent. She could not

give into temptation. She could not do so many things that she wanted to do.

But everyone has a weakness.

————

Her weakness was her father. She had missed him more than anyone else over the past six years. It was like an ache in her chest that sometimes made it difficult to breathe. What would he have been thinking all of this time? How did he manage without her? Did he know she didn't mean for this to happen?

The two of them had been as close as a father and daughter could be and when she saw him by complete accident the previous week on a busy London street, she had stopped dead in her tracks. She never ventured to her old neighbourhood and had purposely moved to the opposite side of the city. Her father shouldn't have been there. This chance encounter shouldn't have happened.

And her father shouldn't have been in a wheelchair.

She couldn't believe it. She wanted to rush to him, to throw her arms around her father. What had happened? Why was he being pushed down the street by someone she didn't recognize?

The urge to see him again was too great. She needed to be close to him, even if she could not let him see her. It was the only thing she could do.

This is how she found herself outside of her old house, the house she had not seen in six years. She loitered about half a block away, pretending to look at her phone, occasionally walking past her old front door and then turning around and walking past it again. She couldn't see anything and her father did not appear. But she knew that her family was still living there. The garden gnome she had picked out seven years earlier at the local garden centre — ridiculed by everyone in her family except her father — was in its usual spot to the right of the front door.

She had been warned not to go back. She had been told of the severe consequences. But what is stronger — fear or love?

Three days later her body was found floating in the canal. She had been warned.

ABOUT THE AUTHOR

JAYE BAILEY is a writer living in London. She is a big fan of true crime and detective fiction and the characters of Luke, Sadie and Hana have been in her head for a long time. Jaye finally decided to put pen to paper and begin the DCI Luke Wiley series.

When she's not writing, Jaye loves to travel. When at home, her house seems to be the destination house of choice for all the neighbourhood cats and, in her humble opinion, she makes the best spaghetti bolognese on the planet. (Yes, she will send you the recipe.)

Find out more at: jayebaileybooks.com

TWO YARDS

Printed in Great Britain
by Amazon

28209077R00158